RUINED BY THE BARON

LEGENDARY LORDS OF THE TON

SUZANNA MEDEIROS

Legends and love collide…

They are the men no woman can tame.
Some whisper about them. Others want to be them.
Known for their wealth, scandalous love affairs, and
the secrets that surround them.
They are the Legendary Lords of the ton.

RUINED BY THE BARON

Forbidden desire…

As the sister of a close friend, Lady Victoria Wright is forbidden. But when she faces an unwanted betrothal to a cruel nobleman, Victoria concocts a scandalous plan to ruin her reputation. And she's chosen me to act as her seducer.

It should be a simple charade. When her reputation lies in tatters, her father will have no choice but to release her from the engagement. But as Victoria plays the role of my mistress, something dangerous ignites between us.

My honorable intentions crumble with each heated glance. Each forbidden touch. Each stolen kiss.

Now I want her for myself. We just need to ensure that her powerful father, who will do anything to have her back, doesn't find her.

To learn about Suzanna Medeiros's future books, you can sign up for her newsletter at: suzannamedeiros.com/newsletter

My protests died when Moreland placed his hands on my cheeks and physically turned me to face him. We remained like that for what seemed like an eternity, his hands cupping my face and our thighs pressed together.

I already knew that his eyes were a light gray—it was impossible not to notice such an uncommon color. But now I could see that darker flecks swirled within them. And as we continued to stare at each other, I could see the way his pupils grew larger. If I were capable of speech, I would have asked him why. It seemed like such an odd thing to notice, but I couldn't help but wonder if something significant was happening between us.

Surely I was imagining things, but the very air that surrounded us seemed to grow thick with tension.

"I'm going to take care of you."

A soft whimper escaped, and I wanted to sink through the floor. *What is wrong with me?*

But the sound seemed to bring about a strange reaction in Moreland. His lids grew heavy, and his face came closer.

The sharp knock at the front door sent both of us scrambling backward.

For my readers.
Thank you for joining me on this exciting new adventure.

Love, Suzanna

CHAPTER 1

BARON MORELAND

APRIL 1820

The three balls were spread across the billiard table as though I'd strategically placed them. I leaned over the table, took a moment to center myself, and drew back my cue with practiced ease.

With a soft clunk, my ball struck the first ball, then the second one. I grinned and straightened as they sailed smoothly across the table's surface and dropped into the corner pockets.

Before I could bask in my win, a broadsheet

landed in the middle of the billiard table. *The Mayfair Chronicle.* It had become something of a ritual with that paper. Not a week passed of late without an article penned by the anonymous Lady X about one of our exploits. Viscount Kendrick leaned against the table and waited for me to pick it up.

"Who is it today?" I scanned the article, searching for my name. When I didn't see it, I returned to the beginning and started reading.

> *This author has it on good authority that one of the Legends may be considering a change in marital status. Not that anyone expects Viscount K to remain faithful to the woman in question (someone from the demimonde, no less!), but it is an interesting development. Will he be the first Legend to fall?*

I didn't even try hiding my amusement. "Mirabelle?"

Viscount Fairfax handed me my winnings, then took the periodical from me.

Kendrick cursed. "She's become nothing but a nuisance. But this?" He waved a hand at the *Chronicle.* "It's definitely time for her to find another protector."

Fairfax clapped him on the shoulder, his eyes twinkling with mirth. "I'm sure you two would have beautiful babies."

Kendrick snatched the broadsheet from him and swore. His annoyance only served to amuse Fairfax more.

"I've been thinking of finding a mistress myself—*not* Mirabelle." I didn't know how Kendrick had found the patience to deal with her for so long. "Someone who knows her place."

Kendrick laughed. "You? You're the king of variety. Why would you give that up?"

I thought about the bruise I currently sported on my backside after last night's activities. "Climbing out of windows in the middle of the night gets tiresome. And truth be told, one body is much the same as another in the dark. It would be a nice change of pace to leave through the front door."

Fairfax straightened, his expression wiped clean of emotion, but I knew him too well. He was trying to mask his amusement. "I would die a happy man if you'd allow me to witness you climbing out a conquest's window. We can forego all this billiard nonsense—I'll give you my money directly."

I glared at him.

Kendrick chuckled. "I wouldn't mind seeing that myself."

I was tempted to knock their heads together. In no world would I allow them to wait outside the bedroom window of some wench I swived. I could concede that the previous night's scene would have given them at least a month of enjoyment as they retold the story to all and sundry, but I was too annoyed to find amusement in having barely escaped the woman's attempt to force me into marriage. Even if her brother had managed to break into the bedroom in time to catch us, I wasn't that honorable. She would have to look elsewhere for a fool to entrap.

Fairfax gave a low whistle, distracting me from my thoughts. He made that sound when he spotted a woman he wanted to get to know better. I raised a brow, and he jerked his head toward the other end of the room. My skin was already prickling with unease when I turned to see who'd caught his attention. Unsure what I expected to see, it wasn't Mr. Clarence guiding a young woman to the stairs that led up to Rexford's private rooms. As club secretary of King's, Clarence was always somewhere around the club, ensuring everything ran smoothly and averting disasters before they could happen. But I'd never seen him escort a woman to the inner sanctum before.

I could see why she'd captured Fairfax's attention, though she was walking away from us. She had dark, almost black hair styled in one of those elaborate displays of curls. She was petite, probably five feet tall, if that, but something about the way she carried herself told me she was a woman of breeding. On those rare occasions when the club was open to the fairer sex, the women who stepped through the front doors were from the demimonde. But I could feel in my bones that this woman wasn't from that world.

"Who do you think she is?" Fairfax's voice was low, interested.

For some reason I couldn't fathom, I wanted to punch him.

The woman chose that moment to glance over her shoulder. Our eyes met, and time stood still. Even from a distance, I saw the almost unnatural deep blue of her eyes, and I couldn't look away.

Fairfax's voice was an unwelcome intrusion. "Why do you think Clarence is taking her upstairs? Do you think Rexford would share?"

Kendrick elbowed him, saving me the trouble. "That's Rexford's sister."

Fairfax gave a disappointed grunt. I was still incapable of speech, caught within the web of the woman's gaze. For some reason, I felt as though she was sizing me up. If she were anyone else, I would have crossed the distance that separated us and introduced myself. Then I would have done everything in my power to ensure she was in my bed that night.

She turned away, and Clarence ushered her upstairs.

"Do you know why she's here?" Thankfully, my voice sounded somewhat normal.

Kendrick shrugged. "No idea. But it must be something important for her to come here. Sherbourne usually keeps his daughter locked away at home."

Of course he did. The Duke of Sherbourne had lost any measure of control over his eldest son and heir. He wouldn't want his daughter to be corrupted by her brother's influence.

"If Rexford's sister is visiting him here, it must concern something serious."

Fairfax's words echoed my curiosity, but in the end, it didn't matter. Rexford's sister was untouchable. I needed to put thoughts of her from my mind.

I forced a casual tone I was far from feeling. "She's beyond our reach." I moved to the billiard table and began racking the balls. "Another game?"

Fairfax grinned. "I'd much rather pay to watch you climb out a small bedroom window. If you can arrange for a husband or father to chase you out, I'll pay double. No, make that triple. It would be worth it."

I walked to the head of the table and lined up my first shot—and missed. Fuck. I never missed.

Fairfax whistled. "It appears today is finally my lucky day."

CHAPTER 2

LADY VICTORIA WRIGHT

I followed Mr. Clarence into my brother's club—King's. I'm not sure how he knew I was arriving, but Mr. Clarence was already waiting when our carriage slowed to a halt before the building.

My maid Lily was with me. She must have sent word ahead. At the beginning of the season, the day after Father and I had arrived in London, she'd confessed that my brother had somehow arranged for her to be hired as my lady's maid. He'd wanted to ensure I had someone close to me who would keep me safe.

I hadn't heard from Rexford in years—Father had made certain of that—but Lily had told me that he'd promised he would always be available if I needed assistance. And that morning, Lily had known I needed Rexford's help.

Thank heavens Father was busy today. The entire staff kept careful watch over me, and I wondered if that was because Father worried that I, too, might escape. But while Rexford had the means to live independently, I was wholly dependent on my father.

When I'd woken that morning, dread had shrouded me like a cloud. My entire world was coming to an end. Father had informed me that he'd made arrangements for my betrothal to the Marquess of Heddington, which meant that at the end of the season, I would be the prisoner of another old and, if rumors were to be believed, cruel man.

But after a short conversation with Lily, I had a glimmer of hope. She'd helped me dress, and I'd informed the staff that I would be going to Bond Street in search of new gloves I simply must have for tonight's ball. While Father's carriage waited outside the shop, Lily had escorted me out the back door into another waiting carriage. I hadn't asked how she'd managed that feat. I didn't really care. All I needed to know was that the carriage would take me to my brother, who would somehow arrange for my freedom.

My smile was shaky as I greeted Mr. Clarence and followed him into the club. At one time, he'd been my father's steward, but he'd left with Rexford and was now helping my brother manage King's.

I was overwhelmed by the enormity of my actions and didn't take in the appearance of the club. He took me through what I assumed was a servant's hallway and up a set of stairs. When we emerged into what was clearly the billiard room, I was relieved to see that the room was nearly empty. The walls were a deep-green color with mahogany wood accents. Four billiard tables occupied the room, one in each corner, but at this hour, only one group of men was playing.

I kept my gaze averted and followed Mr. Clarence to a second set of stairs. Some instinct made me turn to look at the three men in the far corner of the room who laughed among them-selves. I knew without being told that they were Legends. Only my brother's closest friends would be here when the club was closed to the public.

Rexford and his friends were known far and

wide as the Legendary Lords of the ton. Knowing that Rexford was my brother, many young women tried to befriend me, hoping I could share some juicy tidbit of gossip. While I couldn't offer any stories, I'd certainly heard my fair share of rumors from others since arriving in town.

One of the men turned, and I recognized the appraisal in his eyes when he spotted me. He was very pleasing to the eye, and I could imagine many women falling all over themselves to gain his attention. He possessed classically handsome features and fair hair. Even from this distance, I could tell that he knew the effect he had on women.

I turned away and started up the stairs. But some invisible force had me glancing over my shoulder. My gaze collided with one of the other two men, and I froze. Nothing existed but the tall, dark-haired man. For some reason, my heart began to race. That hadn't happened when Father told me I would be marrying Lord Heddington, who had long been a personal friend of his. Nor had it happened when my father arranged for his doctor to examine me yesterday evening to ensure I still possessed my maidenhead.

The situation had been horrifying, but I wasn't surprised. Father had always treated me as nothing more than a shiny piece of fluff to trot out before others. I doubt he considered me a person who possessed emotions. Heaven knows he'd made it his life's mission to eradicate any sign of willfulness.

Thankfully, the doctor's examination had been quick and perfunctory. Lily had been present, of course, standing by my shoulder and watching the man like a hawk to ensure he didn't take any unseemly liberties. I'd simply closed my eyes and pretended I was somewhere else. A lifetime under Father's tutelage had taught me never to reveal a sign of weakness.

But something about the way this stranger looked at me made me feel as though he was seeing into my very soul. It unnerved me.

The spell was broken when Mr. Clarence murmured, "He's waiting."

I turned away with reluctance and followed him up the stairs to my brother's study. Mr. Clarence opened the door after knocking once, and I preceded him into the room.

Rexford rose from his seat behind the desk. I hadn't seen him since he'd escaped Father's control five years ago. I'd been thirteen years old then to his twenty-three. He was no longer the surly young man he'd been back then. An undeniable air of confidence surrounded him. Rexford opened his arms, and I hurried to embrace him. As he pulled me into his chest, I breathed in his scent.

He was the owner of King's and the undisputed head of the Legendary Lords. I'd heard so much gossip about him in the short time I'd been in London. Many thought him wicked, but he was still my brother, and his actions proved that he still cared about me.

He released me and stared down at me. "I'd hoped never to see you here."

Emotion clogged my throat, and I had to force it back. "But you're not surprised."

"No." He trailed a finger along my cheek. "You're a young woman now. You were only thirteen years of age the last time I saw you."

"Thank you for sending Lily to me," I said. "If not for her…" I tried not to think about the unspeakable future that had lain ahead for me this morning.

Rexford shook his head. "That was all Clarence's doing. As Father's steward, Clarence was intimately acquainted with his habits. He explained to me that we needed at least one member on Father's staff who could stay by your side and offer assistance if the need arose."

I turned to thank the older man but realized Rexford and I were alone. I would have to thank him later.

Rexford led me to a set of leather armchairs placed around a small table. Six chairs for the six Legends. I found myself wondering at the many discussions that must have taken place among them in this space. Perhaps they planned out how best to shock society—or how to build my brother's club into the one place in all of London that men were clamoring to join.

He waited for me to sit before settling into a chair next to me. "Tell me what happened."

"You don't know?" Somehow, that surprised me.

He shook his head. "Lily was there to protect you, not to act as a spy. She and Clarence meet periodically so we can ensure you're well. I know they've discussed how best to help you escape Father's control should the need arise. But it's not as though she relays everything you think or do." He reached out to squeeze my hand before dropping it again. "I was afraid Father had poisoned you against me. That I would be the last person you'd come to even if you were in desperate need of help."

He wasn't wrong. "Father tried," I said. "He told me all manner of awful things about how you'd abandoned us and no longer cared about us. But you were always kind to me, even though you were so much older. And that last night before you left, you told me that I could always come to you. I refused to believe you'd changed so much."

"You remembered. I hated leaving you there." His voice was low, soft.

I wondered if anyone besides me had ever seen this side of him.

I nodded. "I did. But fear not, Father was never cruel to me. I don't think he considers me a real person. I was a doll he liked to show off on occasion. But he was never mean."

"What happened?" He tilted his head.

"He wants me to marry Lord Heddington."

Rexford swore, and I couldn't hold back my amused smile. I agreed wholeheartedly.

"The man is as old as Father and far more lecherous."

Something in my brother's tone sent a shiver of dread down my spine. I knew that men could be cruel to women, but the thought of being bound in marriage to someone like that horrified me. I didn't want to think about what it would be like to bear that man's children.

"What happens now? Do you spirit me away? I don't want to marry Heddington, but we both know Father would never allow me to go against his wishes."

Rexford leaned back in his chair and looked off into the distance, his arms crossed. I could almost hear him thinking, going through scenarios as he tried to figure out how best to help me.

"I am more than willing to leave. I could hide in a village and pretend to be a young widow. Or perhaps we can say that my husband is in the military and serving on the continent."

Rexford shook his head. "You would hate that."

I shrugged. "It wouldn't be horrible. Certainly not that different from being hidden away in Father's house most of the time. He only trotted me out on occasion."

"You're out in society this year."

"Yes, that was the occasion. And many men were interested in courting me. I wasn't drawn to anyone in particular, but for Father to choose Heddington without even an ounce of consideration for what I wanted…" I sighed. "I shouldn't have been surprised, but I was."

"It benefits him most," Rexford said. "The marquess is a powerful man. He's wealthy and has a voice in parliament that many listen to. And we both know Father's sole purpose in life is to be the most powerful man in England. He chooses his allies with great care."

"And has no qualms about sacrificing his daughter."

"Or his son," Rexford added. "But I got away, and now you have as well."

"Father won't be happy when he returns home and discovers I'm not there. Do you think he'll come here?"

Rexford smiled. "Oh, he'll definitely pay me a visit, but not right away. When he arrives, you'll already be hidden."

The gleam in his eyes told me he'd settled on a course of action. I placed a hand on his arm. "Where am I going?"

He rested his hand over mind. "Be honest with me, Victoria. Do you merely want to hide from Father? He'll search all of England until he finds you. But you might be able to convince him to give up on his plans altogether."

I'd come here thinking that perhaps my brother could hide me. I'd never considered another option.

If I could make him abandon his plans to marry me to Heddington, I wanted to do it.

"Is that possible? I can't imagine anything that would make him change his mind."

Rexford took careful stock of me as he spoke. "He would abandon you altogether if you were ruined."

My mouth dropped open. "Ruined?" Yesterday's humiliating examination had illustrated just how much Father valued my purity. "Father would be livid."

"Yes." Rexford's grin held an edge of cruel satisfaction.

I had to admit that I could understand the emotion. Father didn't care for either of us. He only cared about what we could do for him. We were extensions of his almighty power. He'd lost control over his heir, which had caused him to tighten his grip on me.

But if I was ruined... My thoughts went immediately to the broad-shouldered, dark-haired man downstairs who'd caught my attention.

"What do I need to do?"

MORELAND

*D*espite my distracted state, I managed to win the game. It was an easy feat since Fairfax was terrible at billiards. He was much better at cards, which meant we traded winnings back and forth. That was fine with me. I was there for the comradery, not to bankrupt my friends.

Clarence joined us shortly after the game finished. Rexford's sister wasn't with him.

"His Lordship requests your presence upstairs."

The three of us must have presented a comical sight, the way we stood there for a few moments just staring at one another. Clearly, no one had a guess about what was happening.

"Are Clifton and Greyson coming?"

"I believe they're in one of the back rooms. I'm on my way to inform them now." Clarence inclined his head, then turned to do just that.

The Earls of Clifton and Greyson were the other Legendary members. We numbered six in total: Rexford, me, Fairfax, Kendrick, Clifton, and Greyson. If he wanted to speak to all of us, that made it a formal meeting.

What could be so important about Rexford's sister that demanded a meeting of the Legends? Perhaps it was just a coincidence.

Fairfax nudged me with his shoulder. "Are you worried that you won't be taking more of my money today? Or are you still thinking about a certain woman?"

"Remember that you're talking about Rexford's sister," Kendrick said.

Fairfax's grin sobered. We all knew that she would be off limits.

As we made our way upstairs, I couldn't suppress my anticipation at the thought of seeing her again. I didn't even know her name. Fairfax knocked, and we entered at Rexford's acknowledgment.

I scanned the room, but his sister wasn't there. Of course not. Why would she need to meet with us? Still, she hadn't departed the same way she'd arrived. So she'd either left via the back entrance, or she was in one of Rexford's rooms. The entire top floor was devoted to Rexford's study and his private chambers. King's was his club, after all.

Rexford didn't speak, but he did move to the sideboard to pour a measure of brandy for us. Six glasses were already laid out.

Clifton and Greyson entered then. Their raised brows and the way they studied us clearly indicated that they, too, had no idea why the meeting had been called. And since they hadn't seen Clarence arrive with Rexford's sister, they were completely in the dark.

We each took a glass from the sideboard and moved to our usual armchairs.

"This is unexpected," Greyson said. "Did something happen that I should be aware of?"

Rexford drained his glass in one swallow and, with exaggerated care, set it on the low table around which the chairs were gathered. I met Fairfax's gaze. The air in the room had developed an electrical charge, and I couldn't help thinking that something momentous was about to happen. Scanning the others, I could tell they felt it too.

"I've had a visit from my sister, who turned eighteen just before the start of the season."

"I'm shocked Sherbourne allowed her out of his sight," Clifton said.

Rexford folded his arms across his chest and leaned back in his chair. "He didn't, but a few members in his household are loyal to me. One of them helped Victoria escape my father's clutches."

Victoria. The beauty had a name, and damn if it didn't make her even more intriguing.

"The duke will be displeased," Clifton continued. "I assume this has to do with his plans for marrying her off?"

Rexford nodded. "She was told last night that he's arranged to marry her off to Heddington. The wedding is supposed to take place at the end of the season."

"Fuck." I drained my glass.

"Indeed," Rexford said.

Kendrick leaned forward. "Your father can't know of his reputation. Surely he wouldn't want his daughter to marry someone with such proclivities."

Fairfax nodded. "And what about that business with his wife supposedly jumping to her death because she was grief-stricken about not bearing children."

"You underestimate my father," Rexford said. "All he cares about is power and money, and Heddington has both. He would have no qualms about using Victoria to cement his friendship with the man."

Fairfax grunted softly in dismay. "I knew your father was unscrupulous but I didn't think he was evil."

"Is she hiding in your rooms?" Fear slid through my veins at the thought. "Surely your father will come here when he discovers her absence. Since she's not yet of age, he'll have the right to remove her from the premises."

Rexford's focus narrowed on me. He had the same eyes as his sister, but hers were spaced more widely. I hadn't realized it when she'd ensnared me in the depths of her gaze earlier, but Rexford's were the same unnatural blue. I wondered if they'd inherited that trait from their mother, who by all accounts had been a beauty. Having seen Victoria, even if only for a moment, I could certainly believe it. The thought of the Marquess of Heddington touching her had me clenching my fists, and I had to force myself to relax.

"Sherbourne will send his men here, yes. They'll try to forcibly remove her."

"So, she's not here," Clifton said.

"She'll be leaving shortly."

I felt a measure of relief. The idea that someone could give their daughter to a man like Heddington was unfathomable.

"But I won't be able to hide her forever. She is still three years from her age of majority. Until she turns twenty-one, if my father finds her, he'll be within his rights to force her to marry whomever he chooses. No one could stop him."

"You'll hide her away in the country?" That made sense to me. Soon, she would be in a carriage, transported far from London by some of Rexford's men. His most trusted, I hoped, because if Rexford had men in his father's employ, I wouldn't be surprised if the reverse was also true.

"I'm looking for volunteers," Rexford said.

"I'll help her escape. And make sure she's safely hidden." I hadn't realized I would offer until the statement was out of my mouth, but I hated the idea of Rexford's sister being forced to marry

Heddington. If I could help her escape, then I knew she would be safe.

"You haven't heard what I have in mind."

"You're asking for volunteers to help her escape London. We've all heard stories about Heddington. I'm sure everyone here would do the same."

There was a strange look on Rexford's face.

A tense silence filled the room, then Fairfax spoke. "What else could you have in mind?"

Rexford steepled his fingers at his waist, his gaze settling on each of us in turn. "The only way to keep her safe, to make sure she is no longer of use to my father, is to ruin her."

Silence settled over us, and I imagined the others were as shocked as I was. Was Rexford saying that he wanted one of us to compromise, then discard, his sister?

Fairfax cleared his throat. "I will gladly sacrifice myself for the cause." I punched his shoulder, and he released a soft grunt. "What? He asked for volunteers."

Rexford looked at me. "Are you still eager to help, Moreland?"

Rexford knew me well enough to know that I would always come to the aid of a friend. But the matter concerning his sister was more than a little unsettling. It would make me the target of a very powerful duke, who would do anything in his power to destroy me. Despite my certainty that the situation would become far more complicated than the simple solution Rexford presented, I couldn't stand the idea of anyone else going near his sister.

I nodded. "I am at your service."

Rexford's gaze remained on me. "If the rest of you could give us a few minutes."

The other men rose to their feet. No one spoke, but each one in turn squeezed my shoulder, communicating their unspoken support, before filing out of the room.

Rexford's eyes remained on me the entire time. When the door closed, he finally spoke. "You don't have to do this. If you have any doubts, I'll understand."

Even if I were so inclined, I wouldn't change my mind. I owed Rexford—all the Legends, really—everything. He knew that, and I respected the fact that he didn't want to force me.

But what he didn't know was that something intangible had taken place downstairs when his sister and I had locked gazes. I wasn't foolish enough to believe in destiny, but I couldn't shake the feeling that I needed to take care of her. The fact that she was Rexford's sister—and that he clearly cared for her—would give me the excuse I needed to offer her my protection.

"I'm sure. But what exactly do you have in mind? And more importantly, how does your sister feel about this?"

He nodded. "I'm impressed that you care."

I couldn't help but bristle. Of course I cared. I may enjoy bed sport, and I never slept with the same woman more than once, but I didn't force my attention on anyone who didn't want it. They came to my bed willingly.

"How do you see this ruination playing out?" I couldn't imagine that Rexford was giving me free rein to bed his sister. Then what would happen? Would I be expected to tell everyone about it?

"Victoria has agreed to become your mistress. You'll set her up in a house—I already have the perfect property. And of course, you'll need to visit her on occasion."

"Of course." Somehow, I kept my tone even, but my palms started to sweat. I'd never kept a mistress. Kendrick's current predicament with his mistress was proof that such a situation was the perfect breeding ground for unwelcome complications. But the thought of spending time with the beautiful young woman who'd ensnared me so easily with just a look had me more than willing to jump in with both feet.

Hopefully a few conversations with Rexford's sister would be enough to curb whatever foolish fantasies I had already envisioned. I normally spent time with women who were my age or older. I would be thirty in two years' time. What would I even have to say to a debutant?

Rexford continued as though he hadn't noticed that my thoughts were in turmoil. "I'll ensure that the rumors reach my father's ears soon enough. He'll blame me, of course, for daring to introduce his prized possession to one of my degenerate companions."

"Of course. And your father will be livid when he realizes that your sister has been ruined by a lowly baron."

Rexford's grin revealed more than a hint of satisfaction. "I look forward to that conversation when he finally decides to face me."

I snorted. If Sherbourne thought Rexford could

be cowed by a verbal dressing down, he clearly didn't know his son.

"Do you think that will be enough to keep her safe?"

Rexford examined me for what felt like an eternity. It took everything I possessed to keep from squirming in my seat.

"I don't need to know details about what happens between you two. As long as it's consensual, it's not my concern."

I nodded. There was no point in denying I wanted to bed his sister. I would do everything in my power to keep that from happening, but I wasn't foolish enough to promise that it wouldn't. "So what happens now?"

"She's waiting in my sitting room. I thought the two of you should speak first. If you are still in agreement afterward, I'll have a carriage take you to the house where you'll be keeping her." He grinned. "It's near my father's house in Mayfair—one of my properties on Grosvenor Square, close enough to drive Sherbourne crazy."

A frisson of unease snaked down my spine. "Will she be safe there?"

"I'll staff the house with trusted servants."

I'd known Rexford since our schoolboy days in

Eton. He'd always been resourceful, yet it still amazed me that he could pull together such a scheme so quickly.

We stood, and I followed him from his study. With every step, and despite my better judgment, anticipation surged through my veins.

CHAPTER 4

As the minutes passed, I grew increasingly unsettled. It was difficult to believe that I could be more worried than when Father had delivered his devastating news about my betrothal. I knew Rexford would take care of me, protect me. But now he was suggesting protection of another sort.

Rexford had escorted me to his small sitting room, where I waited to see how my future would unfold. I shouldn't have been surprised to learn that my brother lived above King's. But I was coming to discover that he was practical as well as resourceful.

The room was smaller than his study and clearly a man's domain, with dark wood furniture and leather armchairs. I imagined he didn't receive callers there. Rexford would conduct his business in his larger study. I sank into one of the two armchairs and tried to calm my pounding heart, but no amount of deep breathing could still my racing thoughts.

What if he didn't want to accept my brother's proposal? I supposed it didn't really matter who ruined me. The beautiful blond man could do it just as easily. A third man had been with them, but I couldn't say what he looked like, because I hadn't been able to tear my gaze from the man who'd caught my attention.

I didn't even know his name.

A brisk knock at the closed sitting room door was all the notification I received before it swung open and Rexford walked into the room. He stood there for a moment, examining me. No doubt he was looking for any indication that I'd changed my mind. He wouldn't find it.

I rose to my feet. "What did he say?"

Rexford stepped aside, and another man entered the room. My dark stranger.

It didn't seem possible, but my heart leaped. Surely such a reaction wasn't normal. I'd been introduced to many men over the past month, and no one had affected me the way this man did.

Rexford turned to him. "Allow me to introduce you to my sister, Lady Victoria Wright. Victoria, this is my good friend Moreland."

Moreland. I searched my memory for the name and hit upon his title after a few seconds. "Baron Moreland. Father will be livid."

I held out my hand, relieved that it wasn't shaking. He took it and dropped a very proper kiss an inch above it. A shiver raced through me. I was wearing gloves, but he wasn't. Something about seeing my small hand in his caused heat to spread through me. I couldn't understand my reaction, but I was saved from the embarrassment of snatching my hand back when he released it.

He clasped his hands behind his back. "It's a pleasure to make your acquaintance, Lady Victoria."

Good heavens, his voice was like nothing I had ever heard before—low, deep. Intimate. I dipped into a shallow curtsy, incapable of replying.

My brother, of course, noticed my state. He

took my hands in his and looked down at me. "If you've changed your mind, you have only to say the word. I can have someone spirit you away from London within the—"

"No." The exclamation was out before he'd finished speaking.

Rexford's brows rose in question.

I took a deep breath and called upon all my training to keep my voice even. "You were correct, of course. Father will never stop looking for me if you try to hide me. I must make myself wholly undesirable if I'm to gain my freedom."

Rexford examined my face for what felt like an eternity. Finally, he nodded and dropped my hands. "You will be safe here for now, but Father will send his men as soon as he discovers you're missing. I have a house he doesn't know about yet. I'll leave the two of you alone to talk while I make further arrangements."

He turned to Moreland, and something unspoken passed between them. Then, with a nod, he left the room. And closed the door.

It was the first time I'd ever been alone with a man to whom I wasn't related. Father didn't even trust the footmen. A maid shadowed me throughout the house when I wasn't in my room.

Moreland watched me carefully, and I couldn't help but wonder if he expected me to change my mind and run after my brother. Or perhaps he expected me to faint. If so, he would soon learn I wasn't quite so fragile. I'd survived all manner of criticism from my father without so much as flinching. I could certainly have a conversation with a man.

A man who's going to ruin you.

That thought should have caused me at least a hint of alarm, but I finally had my emotions in check. I lowered myself into one of the armchairs and watched as he took the other one.

He grasped the arms of the chair and met my gaze. "Lowly baron reporting for duty, my lady."

And just like that, my equanimity vanished. "Oh no, I didn't mean—it's just that you're a baron, and my father… I didn't mean any offense."

I stopped abruptly as a smile spread across his face. He was teasing me. Good heavens, this man was dangerous when he smiled.

I looked away for a moment as I tried to regather my composure. "What did my brother tell you?"

He outlined the facts I'd shared with Rexford, then his next words made my insides turn upside down. "I've been granted the privilege of ruining you."

I froze in place, uncertain as to how I should reply to such a statement. No doubt the act would be similar to what happened between a husband and wife on their wedding night. At least I wouldn't have to suffer the attentions of Lord Heddington in that area. A lifetime of etiquette coaching in how to conduct myself appropriately in all situations had left me ill prepared to deal with this one.

"I'm glad you were amenable to the idea."

Moreland shrugged. "I owe your brother more than I could ever repay."

His reply felt like the cruelest of set-downs. I didn't know why, precisely, but it bothered me that he was doing this as a favor to my brother. As though that could be the only reason he would speak to me. Had I mistaken that moment we'd shared downstairs when our eyes met. Could it have been one-sided?

Perhaps I should have chosen the blond man instead. He'd clearly been interested, and who knows, he might have made the situation more pleasant than it was turning out to be. "I hope it won't be too much of a sacrifice to spend time in my company."

The words were sharper than I'd intended, and the way Moreland's eyes widened told me that I'd surprised him. Good. If he thought he was dealing with a scared little mouse, then he was mistaken. Yes, I'd been forced to do my father's bidding, but I'd developed a great deal of fortitude because of it. Otherwise, my own sense of self would have disappeared under his inflexible rule. Would someone meek and mild have even considered escaping the way I did?

I straightened my shoulders and held his gaze. "You are clearly the elder here." I put exaggerated emphasis on the word "elder" since I doubted this man was yet thirty years of age.

I'd clearly amused him. One corner of his mouth turned up, but he allowed me to continue. My opinion of him rose. Usually, men loved to jump in and explain things, assuming I had no knowledge beyond how to dress and smile. But in this case, I needed his guidance.

"I'm sure you've had mistresses before and have probably ruined all manner of women, so I shall defer to your expertise."

His smile evaporated. "As I said before, I owe your brother more than you can imagine. So, yes, our arrangement will be known, and everyone will come to think of you as my mistress. But I have no intention of actually ruining you. I'll visit the house your brother has arranged to keep you in, and I'll spend an appropriate amount of time there. But no actual *ruining* will take place."

CHAPTER 5

Victoria stiffened. "I suppose I should thank you for your consideration."

Damn it all to hell. I had expected Rexford's sister to feel reassured that I intended to behave honorably. But instead, she seemed to take offense.

My fists clenched on the chair arms. This arrangement was going to be more difficult than I first thought. I was determined to fulfill my promise to Rexford to keep his sister safe, and that included keeping her safe from me.

He clearly cared for her. He'd risked much when he'd broken away from his father's influence, but Sherbourne was content to wait him out. Rexford was his heir, after all. He would expect his son to return to the fold at some point. But taking Victoria away was another matter entirely. Sherbourne would move heaven and earth to get her back, and Rexford would feel the pressure. I had no doubt Rexford could withstand whatever pressure his father exerted, but I refused to add to his worries by debauching his sister.

"Despite what you might have heard," I said, "we are not all dishonorable reprobates who cannot control ourselves."

"I never thought you were."

She looked away, and I couldn't tell if she was speaking the truth. But it didn't matter. She'd grown up under Sherbourne's thumb, so I was sure she knew that even supposedly honorable men were anything but.

"Should we find someone else?" she asked.

It was my turn to stiffen.

But before I could speak, she continued. "Perhaps the fair-haired gentleman downstairs would be more willing to take on this onerous task."

"No." The denial was out before I'd thought to moderate my tone. "Rexford told me that you asked for me."

She met my gaze again, and the hint of anger in her eyes was unmistakable.

"Why me?" I asked.

I'm not sure what I imagined she'd say. I expected her to refuse to answer or perhaps make a coy reply. It was how any other woman would have answered my question, and heaven knew I'd been in the company of many.

Instead, she let out a soft breath. "I don't know. I thought we shared a moment…" Her voice trailed off, and she shrugged. "I couldn't imagine trying to do this with anyone else."

Her words were a balm to my ego. She didn't want Fairfax. I wasn't sure I could be trusted with that knowledge since heaven knew I found Rexford's sister tempting. But it soothed the jealousy that had sprung to life within me.

"I will endeavor to be worthy of your trust," I said. "I know this entire situation is difficult, and for what it's worth, I admire your strength of will."

She smiled. I wasn't sure when I'd last received such genuine warmth from a woman. I was accustomed to coy flirtation. But for some unknown reason, the fact that I'd elicited this reaction from Victoria caused a spark of happiness to unfurl within me. That made me realize I was in deeper trouble than I could have imagined.

One brisk knock sounded at the door, then it opened. Rexford stood in the doorway, his gaze taking in the way we sat in separate chairs, our bodies angled toward each other. His expression remained impassive, but I realized he'd been testing me to see if I could be trusted alone with his sister.

I couldn't blame him for his caution, and I was determined to be worthy of the trust he'd placed in me.

"The carriage is ready," he said. "I thought it would be best if you two arrived together in Moreland's carriage. No one will believe Victoria is your mistress if I'm seen with you."

Victoria stood, and I did the same. She gave me a small smile, and I inclined my head in reply.

The situation had me on edge. I'd never kept a mistress, and it seemed particularly cruel that this woman would be my first. I wouldn't be able to touch her despite the fact that every part of me demanded I do just that.

She took Rexford's arm, and I followed them down the back stairs to where Rexford had set up his private stables. He'd always enjoyed his conveniences, and in that moment, I finally understood why he'd been adamant about acquiring the lease to the stables, despite how much it had cost. It provided him with a measure of privacy from prying eyes, which meant he could come and go at will without being observed.

He handed Victoria into the carriage, then turned to face me. "The driver and the footman are mine, and a few outriders will follow at a distance. Anyone who observes you will believe the carriage is traveling alone. But if our father has learned about Victoria's disappearance, he will already be searching for her."

I nodded and clapped him on the shoulder. "No harm will come to her."

CHAPTER 6

VICTORIA

The carriage door closed, and Moreland and I were alone. He sat opposite me, his broad chest and shoulders seeming to take up all the room in the small space. His gaze was a physical weight as the tense silence lengthened.

I looked away, smoothing my hand over the dark leather of the bench seat. Together with the dark mahogany wood, it made the interior feel comfortable and welcoming. I could imagine myself stretching out along the seat and sleeping while it carried me far from my troubles.

It was so different from what I was accustomed to. Instead of rich wood, Father's carriages were an homage to gold, and the benches were covered with royal-blue fabric and plush cushions. It was designed to feel ostentatious, and I knew it made him feel important. As a duke, no one would question his position in society, but he thrived on flaunting what he saw as his superiority.

Moreland's carriage was dark, where my father's was bright. My gaze moved to the black curtains, and I couldn't help but wonder how dark the interior would be if I were to draw them—which, of course, made Moreland's presence even more overwhelming. He could do all manner of things to me now, and no one would know.

The thought made me lightheaded.

"Breathe, Lady Victoria. Everything will be fine."

I met his gaze and could see the very real concern reflected there. I hadn't even realized I was holding my breath until I took in great lungsful of air, relishing the way it made the darkness recede from the edges of my vision.

Of all the indignities I'd endured, why did this one seem so insurmountable? "I'm frightened."

I didn't realize I'd spoken aloud until Moreland replied with a soft, "I know. But I promise we'll keep you safe. Just lie back and close your eyes. No harm will befall you while I'm with you."

For some reason, I believed him. I leaned back against the cushions—which were surprisingly comfortable—and closed my eyes. Something about Moreland's presence made me feel safe.

Rexford had readily agreed when I'd mentioned the large man I'd seen downstairs. His expression hadn't shown a flicker of doubt that Moreland could be trusted to carry out our outrageous plan. If Rexford trusted Moreland, then I could as well.

I wasn't sure how long we remained like that. Certainly not long enough to be safely at the edge of town, where I imagined men normally kept their mistresses. But the carriage was already slowing when a horrible thought occurred to me.

I opened my eyes, straightened, and forced myself to ask the question I didn't want him to answer. "Please tell me you don't already have a mistress. Would others believe that you have two mistresses?"

I reconsidered the absurd question I'd just asked. Of course they would. He was one of the

Legendary Lords, and their exploits were well known. I'd never really paid attention to the details since I didn't want to risk reading something about my brother that I didn't want to know. But for some reason, I hated the thought that Moreland might go from visiting me, his pretend mistress, to another woman's bed.

I frowned at the amusement in his expression.

"I've never kept a mistress. You'd be the first."

Curiosity, and a healthy measure of relief, swept through me. I wanted to ask him why, but the carriage was already stopping.

Moreland leaned forward. "Did your brother tell you where we were going?"

I shook my head and looked out the window. I couldn't hold back my gasp. "We're in Grosvenor Square. This can't be where Rexford expects us to stay."

I could imagine the scene. We were so close to Father's grand house in Mayfair that he could storm here on foot. How long would it take? Five minutes perhaps? Not that Father would ever deign to walk. He would have his carriage make the trip. But perhaps not the one with the ducal crest emblazoned on the door. He wouldn't want to announce his presence. He would want to snatch me away before anyone discovered what was happening. Then he would lock me in my room.

"Please tell me that this is just a short stop on our way to the actual destination."

A footman moved into position by the door, but he didn't open it yet.

I closed my eyes and forced myself to take a deep breath. "Grosvenor Square. Father will have me back home by nightfall."

Moreland leaned forward and grasped my hands. I opened my eyes and stared into his, anchoring myself in the calm certainty reflected there.

"Security is already in place here," he said. "Rexford stationed men within the house and outside. You can rest assured that everyone he's employed can be trusted."

I couldn't hold back my laughter. "My father staffed his house with people he thought he could trust."

"But he never accounted for Rexford's cunning."

I shook my head. "My brother managed to sneak Lily into my father's stronghold."

Moreland squeezed my hands. "That won't happen here. Rexford is far too smart for that.

Remember, your father is used to people doing whatever he wants without question. That leads to a carelessness your brother doesn't possess."

I wanted to believe Moreland. I'd given myself fully to this scheme, so I needed to trust that he and Rexford had the situation well in hand. But I wasn't ready for another potential situation that hadn't occurred to me until that moment. I lowered my voice. "I know some of the people who live here. If they see me leaving this carriage with you—"

He shrugged, continuing to hold my hands as he stared into my eyes. "Hopefully, they're looking out their windows right now. That is the plan. We need to ruin your reputation."

I took a deep breath. Yes, that was the plan. I hadn't expected it to be quite so public. But what better way to ruin me than to have my protector set me up in a house where someone I knew could see me? I could do this. I *needed* to do this, and I was determined not to be afraid. This was the only way to gain my freedom. "How should we proceed?"

Moreland released my hands and straightened. "I'm going to exit first, then I'll help you down. It's only a few steps to the house, so we won't be outside long. I'm going to lean down and whisper something. You should laugh or smile. If anyone is watching, they'll need to believe that you want to be with me."

I nodded. "I think I can manage that."

There would be no more hiding, no more pretending I was still locked safely away at home. I pasted a smile on my face—the one I wore whenever Father paraded me before his friends. When he wanted me to act the role of the perfect daughter. Then I leaned a little closer and allowed genuine warmth to show. I couldn't say why, but I trusted Moreland.

He stared back at me, no doubt trying to decide whether my performance would be sufficient. Finally, with a nod, he reached for the door handle. I watched him unlatch it and step down. When he turned back to me, the smile on his face caused my heart to stop—then race. A hint of devilry lit his eyes, a certain teasing quality.

This was all for show, I told myself. He was doing Rexford a favor.

It was ridiculously easy to return that smile and place my hand in his to allow him to help me down. He tucked my arm into his elbow, and I leaned a little closer to him, our bodies almost touching as I smiled up at him.

We stood like that for several seconds, and

despite my certainty that he was dawdling to increase the likelihood of someone seeing us, I didn't care. For the first time in my life, I was intrigued by a man who was showing me attention. This was a game I was used to playing.

He leaned down. "I think we're being watched."

I laughed up at him, and through barely moving lips, I said, "We should put on a good show."

He caressed my chin with the thumb of his free hand, then pressed it against my lower lip. My breath hitched. No one had ever dared to touch me in such a way, and I liked it more than I should.

He turned us toward the house, and we crossed the short distance to the front door, which was already open. As soon as we entered the house and the butler closed the door behind us, Moreland dropped my arm and stood back. I was oddly bereft at the loss of his nearness and couldn't help but feel that I had lost the possibility of something I hadn't even known I wanted.

"My lady."

I turned at the sound of the woman's voice to see Lily standing there, smiling.

"I'm so happy you made it here safely."

I hadn't seen her since she'd handed me over to Mr. Clarence, and I was relieved she, too, was safe. I gave her a quick hug. "Thank you. I'm so glad you're here."

Lily shuddered. "I don't think I would be welcomed back into your father's house."

I didn't want to imagine what Father would do to my maid if he were to see her again. He probably wouldn't recognize her, but others on his staff would. "I owe you my life."

She smiled. For the first time, I saw a woman and not just a servant. And I had to admit that I felt a measure of shame. I'd always liked Lily, but I'd kept her at a distance, assuming that her loyalty was foremost to my father.

Moreland cleared his throat, and I turned to meet his gaze.

"You should go upstairs and get settled." Gone was the man whose primary concern had been to ease my worries.

The new distance in his demeanor saddened me. "You're leaving?"

He shook his head. "I'll wait an hour. Appearances must be kept, after all. I can't drop off my new mistress and leave immediately."

Why was it so difficult for me to remember that Moreland was doing this for my brother and not because he wanted to spend time with me?

"I understand." I turned and followed Lily upstairs.

I would not be disappointed. Today was just another day in the life of a woman whose existence had never truly been her own.

CHAPTER 7

MORELAND

To say I had a restless night's sleep after returning to my townhouse wouldn't come close to the reality. Somehow, in the span of twenty-four hours, I'd gone from being able to do whatever I wanted with whomever I wished to a man who possessed a mistress he couldn't touch. In the past, whenever I was at loose ends, I would have sought comfort in the arms of a willing woman. But now that I had to ensure the entire world believed I was keeping the Duke of Sherbourne's daughter as my paramour, I wouldn't be able to find solace in another. Not so soon, at any rate.

The fact that the only woman I wanted to bed was Victoria was something I tried my best to forget. She was Rexford's sister and untouchable. What we were doing was a charade only, designed to keep her safe.

I'd woken early and headed to Gentleman Jackson's establishment, where I was currently trying to take my frustrations out on my hapless opponent. The bell rang, signaling the end of the match, and I dropped my hands and forced myself to step back. I wasn't quite so far gone that I would pummel the man who had been on the wrong side of my aggravation that morning. At least he was a sturdy enough fellow and would recover quickly.

He'd even managed a few good blows of his own. I shook his hand, and we parted company. I'd only taken a few steps when I saw that Kendrick was waiting for me. He fell into step next to me, and we made our way to where I could get cleaned up.

"It's never a good sign when I find you here so early in the day," he said.

I grunted. I could say nothing to dispute that fact.

Kendrick lowered his voice when we reached the dressing room. "It seems you've joined the club of unfortunate souls who possess a mistress that can't stay out of the *Chronicle*."

My steps faltered. I turned and allowed my gaze to sweep around the room. It was normal enough to have people watching as we engaged in matches, but today, every eye in the room continued to track my progress. I was surprised by how much their knowing looks bothered me. I was used to being the subject of gossip and speculation, but today, their attention was unwelcome. I itched to punch the smirks from their faces.

I turned back to Kendrick. "Don't tell me that Mirabelle is still your mistress. I thought that after yesterday's article, you'd have ended the arrangement."

He snorted. "Of course I did. That's why I'm up so early. I've just come from letting her know that she'll need to leave the house at the end of the month and find another protector."

I raised my brows. "You're being generous."

"I'm not a monster," he said. "I'm not about to cast a woman out into the streets, no matter her profession. I'm sure she'll find someone soon enough. But we're not here to talk about me."

Every muscle in my body tightened, and I felt the need to hurry. I walked over to where my valet waited for me in the far corner of the dressing room and began the ritual of making myself presentable again while Kendrick waited. My valet didn't particularly like coming here, but he'd resigned himself to the fact that pugilism was a sport I enjoyed. It also had the benefit of strengthening my reputation as someone to be reckoned with. My valet moved through the task with practiced ease. I trusted the man but not with someone else's secrets, and so I didn't say a word until he'd finished tying my cravat.

Dismissing him, I turned to Kendrick. "What does it say? Do you have the paper?"

He shook his head. "No, I haven't seen the article yet. Mirabelle, of all people, told me about it, but I have no idea how she already knew."

This was bad. I hadn't expected news of our liaison to spread so quickly. "Were we named?"

"Not outright, but you're the only Legend whose name starts with the letter M. And the daughter of a duke who was supposed to marry a marquess whose first wife died under suspicious circumstances." His eyes met mine. "It won't be long before everyone realizes they're talking about Sherbourne's daughter."

I nodded. "That's what we wanted."

"Yes, it is. But I don't think I have to tell you that the duke is no doubt already tearing the city apart to find her. And he'll punish you for this."

I knew that. Fortunately, I wasn't afraid of Rexford's father. He could try his worst, and he would be surprised to learn I was well insulated against his attempts at revenge.

But I was worried about Victoria. "I need to head to the house and make sure she's all right."

Kendrick raised a brow. "Do you really think he'll want anything to do with her after this?"

It was my turn to snort. "He might not want her back, but that doesn't mean he won't want to punish her. He could lock her away in one of his country houses and wait for the scandal to die down. Once everyone forgets and turns to the next inevitable scandal, he'll be able to marry her off to someone else. A number of decrepit lords who no longer come to town would be able to do whatever they wanted to her in private."

Kendrick stopped and stared at me. "I hadn't considered that."

It had occurred to me, as well as any manner of other horrible things the duke might do to his daughter. I needed to see her right away and ensure she was safe.

CHAPTER 8

VICTORIA

The day started much like every other day. I became aware of Lily moving about my bedchamber, performing her customary actions prior to helping me dress for the day. I lay in bed and listened to her, taking comfort in the familiarity of our routine.

She poured fresh water into the washstand bowl, then moved to my dressing table, where she opened the top drawer to take out the brushes and hairpins she would use to pin up my hair. When she shifted to the wardrobe to select an item of clothing, everything that had happened yesterday came flooding back.

All my belongings were still at my father's house, but Rexford had anticipated every one of my needs. Or at least, I assumed it was my brother who had arranged for the trunk filled with dresses and under-garments that had arrived last night.

I lay there with my eyes closed, remembering every detail of yesterday's escape and waiting for panic to set in. I had completely upended my life. I was no longer Lady Victoria Wright, daughter to the Duke of Sherbourne. Today, I was a ruined woman, another man's mistress.

A smile spread across my face, bone-deep relief sweeping through me. I had spent my whole life trying to make Father happy—and when that didn't seem possible, I tried to stay out of his way. But I had never had an opportunity to discover who I was outside of my relationship to him.

I rose from the bed and greeted Lily, who waited patiently by the dressing table. She smiled back at me. Today, I began my new life.

After dressing I had my breakfast downstairs in the breakfast room, something I never did at home. Normally, I had a light meal brought up to my bedroom since I ate alone.

Father only spent time with me when he needed something, and usually, it was to inform me about what he expected from me before an outing. Today, there would be no trips to Bond Street, and no trips to the lending library to see what new novels might be in circulation. There would be no calls from acquaintances. The few women I'd begun to consider friends would turn their backs on me now, refusing to acknowledge my existence.

But that thought didn't really bother me, because I would make new friends. Lily, for one. The unassuming young woman, who was only a few years older than I, had always been reserved and proper when she'd served as my maid. But now, freed from the constraints of trying to appear as the perfect lady's maid for a duke's daughter, she seemed much younger, and certainly freer with her opinions. I quite liked this version of Lily. The old Victoria Wright would never think of calling a servant a friend. And while we weren't there yet, I felt we were headed in that direction.

After breakfast, I made my way to the small library in the back of the house in search of something to read to pass the time. I settled in the drawing room, telling myself that I was *not* waiting for Moreland's arrival.

It was a dry tome, but it served to pass the time since I didn't have anything else to do. My paints weren't here, and I had nothing with which to draw. I had no preparations to make for visiting friends or attending any entertainment that evening. The day stretched before me, empty of duties and expectations. While I felt a twinge of guilt at not being productive, a small part of me enjoyed the fact that I was free to be as selfish with my time as I wanted.

When I heard a key turning in the front door lock, I couldn't help but worry that Father had somehow found me. I held my breath as the door opened. A footman had gone to intercept whoever it was.

I let out my breath when I recognized Moreland's voice. My gaze went to the clock above the mantelpiece. It was only two in the afternoon. He wasn't supposed to arrive until early evening. That was the schedule we'd decided on last night. He would call and spend a few hours here to keep up the appearance of a man visiting his mistress.

I set the book on the end table and stood, folding my arms at my waist. When Moreland stepped into the doorway, peace settled over me.

But that sense of calm evaporated when I saw the look on his face. "Is something the matter?"

He closed the distance between us. "I have news."

My insides twisted. "You've changed your mind." Of course he had. He'd arrived to tell me that he didn't want to continue with our pretense. "I don't blame you. My father is a powerful man. I know very well what hell befalls those who cross him."

When he scowled, I pressed my lips firmly together. I was babbling, something I hadn't done in years, because it annoyed Father. He'd disciplined that nervous habit out of me years ago.

The silence stretched for several seconds before he shook his head. "No, I haven't changed my mind. I gave you my word."

He'd given my brother his word, but who was I to quibble about semantics? Especially when I was the one benefiting most from the arrangement.

He inclined his head to the settee. "Have a seat, please."

Apparently, my manners had fled. We had both been cast into this unusual situation, but that didn't mean I should throw away all social niceties.

"Of course. I'll just ring for tea—"

"Sit down, Victoria."

He'd called me Victoria, not Lady Victoria. If

his goal was to shock me into silence, it worked. I lowered myself onto the edge of the settee and waited for him to settle into one of the two armchairs placed across from where I sat. Instead, he sank onto the settee next to me.

He'd left space between us, but nothing about sitting this close to an unmarried man could be called respectable—a handsome man who was filled with vitality and to whom I was very much attracted. An image popped into my mind that threatened to steal my breath. Moreland leaning toward me, closing that negligible amount of space, and pressing his mouth against mine.

"I apologize for distressing you just now."

The image faded, and for a disorienting moment, I couldn't remember to what he was referring. "Your news," I said finally.

His gaze hadn't left mine, and it felt as though he was trying to see right through me.

"I've learned that news of our arrangement has made it into the gossip columns."

I gasped. "Which ones?"

His brows drew together. "I was told the news secondhand. Why?"

My heart raced in earnest. "Father reads *The Mayfair Chronicle*."

"Of course he does." Moreland rolled his eyes.

We both knew why Father chose to read the gossip column in that particular newspaper. He hated that Rexford had escaped his control and was obsessed with any news related to his son. *The Mayfair Chronicle* had taken a particular interest in Rexford, giving his circle of friends the moniker by which everyone now knew them. The Legendary Lords of the ton.

Every time Father read that paper, his mood soured. And since news about their exploits was an almost daily event, he was always in a foul mood.

He would be apoplectic with rage when he learned that I was being kept as one of their mistresses. It also meant that Moreland's life could be in danger. That distressing thought hadn't occurred to me until that moment.

"We need to stop this. I should have taken up Rexford's offer to hide me away in the country."

Moreland shook his head. "We've already discussed this. We both know that your father could explain away your sudden absence. Manufacture a family emergency while he turned England upside down looking for you."

I closed my eyes, but I couldn't deny the truth of Moreland's words.

"And when he found you, he would continue with his plans undeterred."

After I'd had a chance to recover from the beating he would no doubt give me. But he would be careful not to mar my face or arms. He wouldn't want to damage the property he intended to barter for a powerful alliance. But he would have no such qualms when it came to Moreland.

"I'm afraid for your safety."

He barked out a laugh, and I wanted to shake him. Couldn't he see that he was in danger?

"Victoria—"

"You're not safe. You might think you are because Father has done nothing to hurt Rexford. But my brother is his heir. Father labors under the mistaken impression that he can still bring him to heel. But you… He would have no misgivings about doing whatever was necessary to hurt the man who dared to impugn the family's honor."

His face softened. "Not your honor?"

This time I laughed. "*His* honor. We are but walking, talking extensions of his name. Rexford has some leeway because he is a man. Men are allowed to sow their oats, get into all manner of scrapes in their youth, but all is forgiven when they wish to return to the fold."

Moreland shook his head. "Rexford will never return to the fold."

"Perhaps not, but he will become the next Duke of Sherbourne. And no one will care what he did before that time—or after, for that matter. He has full impunity. But me?" With each word, I became more convinced about the futility of this whole exercise. "Father will have you killed for trying to ruin me and thwart his plans."

"He can try, but I'm an excellent shot. And I can hold my own with a blade."

This time, I feared my laughter held more than a hint of hysteria. "You think he'll call you out? No, there are other ways to take a man's life." I'd read more than a few horrid novels, and in that moment, I could recall every ghastly death that had befallen those who'd wandered into the wrong place at the wrong time.

"Victoria—"

"No, we must stop this now. There's still time if our names weren't mentioned…"

My protests died when Moreland placed his hands on my cheeks and physically turned me to face him. We remained like that for what seemed like an eternity, his hands cupping my face and our thighs pressed together.

I already knew that his eyes were a light gray—it was impossible not to notice such an uncommon color. But now I could see that darker flecks swirled within them. And as we continued to stare at each other, I could see the way his pupils grew larger. If I were capable of speech, I would have asked him why. It seemed like such an odd thing to notice, but I couldn't help but wonder if something significant was happening between us.

Surely I was imagining things, but the very air that surrounded us seemed to grow thick with tension.

"I'm going to take care of you."

A soft whimper escaped, and I wanted to sink through the floor. What was wrong with me?

But the sound seemed to bring about a strange reaction in Moreland. His lids grew heavy, and his face came closer.

The sharp knock at the front door sent both of us scrambling backward.

CHAPTER 9

MORELAND

Fearing that Sherbourne might have discovered where his daughter was staying, I rose to my feet and positioned myself between her and the front door. It was already opening, and I had no time to send her upstairs.

Victoria also rose, but she remained behind me. Rexford could trust his men here. The same guard who'd intercepted my arrival was moving past the drawing room door to see who had come. I tensed, preparing to join him if Sherbourne had sent his men.

Rexford paused in the doorway, taking in the scene.

Victoria peered around me and let out a soft laugh. I could hear the relief in her voice when she spoke.

"I think we both expected that Father had discovered where I'm staying."

Rexford raised a brow. "Is that why Moreland looks ready to tear me apart?"

I shrugged. "You asked me to keep her safe."

"Indeed."

The dry note in his voice told me that he suspected more was happening here than I was willing to acknowledge. But his timely interruption had shaken some sense back into me.

Rexford stepped into the room, and I took the opportunity to move to one of the armchairs. We waited for Victoria to sit before doing the same. This time, Rexford sat next to his sister.

"I take it that the two of you heard about the article in *The Mayfair Chronicle*?"

Victoria made a soft sound of distress. "Father will have seen it, then. Was I named?"

Rexford looked at me. "Did you see it?"

I shook my head. "No. But Kendrick told me."

Rexford turned to his sister. "No names were

mentioned, of course, but enough details were given as well as first initials. It won't take the duke long to realize the article is about you and Moreland."

"What do we do now?" Victoria asked. "Should we hide?"

I hated the panic in her eyes. A protective instinct that urged me to draw her close, to do everything in my power to comfort her, welled up in me. Fortunately, I was too far away to succumb. Instead, I watched her reach for her brother's hand.

"I think we need to continue with the plan you discussed with Rexford. This article came sooner than we expected, but it works in our favor."

Victoria nodded, and I could see the way she called on all her training to be the perfect wife for another duke or marquess. Her shoulders straightened, and she took a deep breath, clasping her hands in her lap.

Rexford frowned. "If you've changed your mind—"

She shook her head. "No, absolutely not. This is the only way to keep Father from giving me to Heddington. When this is over, I can take another name, perhaps pretend to be a widow, and retire somewhere in the country."

"You'll have our protection," I said.

Rexford met my gaze, and I realized he could see that I wasn't detached about this situation.

"Yes, as Moreland says, we will always be here to protect you."

She smiled at him, then at me, and the power of her gratitude affected me in a way I refused to dwell on.

Rexford leaned back and folded his arms across his chest. "So, you have a choice. You can stay here and wait, or we can escalate our plan."

Victoria's brows drew together. Rexford glanced at me, and I nodded. I knew exactly what he was thinking.

"There is a ball," I said. "It's held monthly and—"

"A ball?" Victoria drew back as if I'd struck her. "I can't attend a ball. Everyone I know will be there."

I leaned forward, hating the distance that separated us. "No, you misunderstand. This is a ball for members of the demimonde. Some of the gentlemen you know might be there, but it is a masked ball. Even if they recognize you, they won't approach you as long as I'm at your side."

She nodded. "But they will talk about it afterward. News will spread."

I waited as she considered my suggestion. I couldn't sway her final decision, but I wanted to see this through with her. I couldn't say why, but something about Victoria, who had just come out in society, affected me more than any other woman I'd known. I couldn't act on my interest, of course. She was Rexford's sister. But that didn't mean I wanted to see anyone else ruin her.

"We can do this," I said. "I give you my word that nothing untoward will happen to you." I could promise her nothing less. Not with her brother sitting right there, watching me carefully.

Victoria let out a soft breath. "I could try to hide, but as you reminded me before Rexford arrived, Father would tear the country apart looking for me. And I can't just hide in here. People need to see me. I must make myself wholly unsuitable as a wife for one of Father's friends."

I met Rexford's gaze, and I could tell that he wass thinking the exact same thing as me. Victoria would never really be safe. She might be ruined as a wife, but if Sherbourne was as ruthless as his reputation painted him, nothing would prevent him from selling his daughter as a mistress. Even after she was ruined, she would always need to hide.

"I'll see to the plans." Rexford stood, his visit clearly at an end.

Victoria and I also stood.

Rexford took both her hands in his. "I'll arrange for you to visit a modiste who can see that you are properly attired for the ball."

Inappropriate images filtered through my head. I was a regular attendee at those balls, and usually, the women showed a great deal of skin. I sincerely hoped that Victoria's dress would be on the more modest side.

I offered her what I hoped was a reassuring smile. "I know that Rexford will see to your safety, but I'd feel better if I went with you."

Victoria wrapped her arms around her middle. "Is it safe for me to remain here, so close to Father's house?"

"I'll stay here until you feel more comfortable."

I didn't know what possessed me to make that offer, but her obvious relief was reward in itself.

"Since the matter is settled…" Rexford said, interrupting the moment that passed between me and his sister. "Walk me outside, Moreland."

Chastened, I gave Victoria another reassuring

nod and followed Rexford from the house. He took precisely three steps away from the front door, then turned to face me.

"I don't want to know any details, but if you hurt her, I'll kill you myself."

My first instinct was to reassure him that nothing would ever happen between me and his sister, but I couldn't make myself say the words. They would be a lie, after all. I'd been alone with Victoria for only a few minutes, and I'd almost kissed her.

I nodded. "She is safe with me."

I only prayed that I could keep my word.

CHAPTER 10

VICTORIA

A sense of loss settled over me when Moreland left with my brother, which I recognized was absurd. Moreland was loyal to Rexford and would always choose him over me. We'd known each other less than a day, after all. But I couldn't deny that I'd gained great comfort from his promise to take care of me.

The way he'd looked at me when we were sitting together, the way he'd leaned toward me... My foolish romantic whim had led me to believe he might kiss me. But now, away from the magnetism of his personality, I realized I'd imagined his interest. Moreland would never do anything to raise my brother's ire. Still, I couldn't ignore the longing that washed over me as the front door closed behind them.

I hesitated, unsure what to do. What if Rexford needed Moreland to do something else for him? I could go upstairs and ask Lily to keep me company. I'd enjoyed getting to know her better yesterday. I'd noticed the above-average number of footmen my brother had hired and knew they would keep me safe. I wanted Moreland's company, but I didn't *need* him.

I waited several more seconds. Then, with a shake of my head, I left the drawing room. I'd just started climbing the stairs when the front door opened. I whirled, my stomach swooping.

It was Moreland.

I could hear Rexford's carriage pulling away, and relief flooded me that Moreland hadn't gone with him.

"You returned."

He seemed surprised to see me there and stared at me, a slight V forming between his brows. "I promised I would."

Had he? My emotions were so muddled. Fear, yes, but mixed with a healthy dose of something new and unexpected. Evidently, when it came to Moreland, my usual sense of preservation was nowhere to be found.

"I thought that perhaps Rexford needed to call you away."

He shook his head. "No, he just wanted to make sure you were well. He feared you were putting on a brave face for him."

I didn't know what to say to that, because my brother was correct. The entire situation was overwhelming for someone who'd spent their entire life being told that they needed to be circumspect in all things. It had never even occurred to me that I could choose my future.

With anyone else, I wouldn't admit the truth. But Moreland wasn't just anyone. "This is more difficult than I thought it would be."

His features softened. "I imagine this is the first time you've done anything to thwart your father's will."

I smiled lightly. "That you know about."

His eyes crinkled, his amusement clear. "What could you possibly have done that went against your father's wishes?"

I shrugged. In truth, my small rebellions were nothing to brag about. "I read novels when Father dictated that my reading material should be dedicated to subjects that would improve my mind. Things that would make me an asset to someone he deemed worthy of marrying me."

He must have sensed there was more because he waited for me to continue.

"And occasionally, when he was gone—usually on those days when he was in parliament—Lily and I would sneak from the house and go to Hatchard's Bookshop. I always came home with music that would prove to him I was dedicated to improving my skill at the pianoforte for my future husband's pleasure, and books on proper household management. But I hoarded those novels as a small treasure."

I couldn't help but wonder if Father would find them now. If he tore my room apart—or more likely, he would have a servant do it—they would find the books. Would he care? The whole world would soon learn that I was Moreland's mistress. No doubt he would see those novels as evidence that my mind had been warped by what he called romantic nonsense.

Silence stretched between us, and I didn't know what to do. I wasn't actually his mistress. He was only here because of his loyalty and friendship to my brother.

I straightened and forced myself to say, "If you have somewhere else you need to be—"

He shook his head. "Nothing is more important than my duty to you."

Duty. I frowned at the word. Of course, he would see me as a chore to be handled.

He continued. "I would appreciate it if you could show me to the study or the library. I have a few notes to write, to people who were expecting to see me today. I need to inform them I'm busy elsewhere."

I shrugged. "I don't know if there's a study. I haven't explored the entire house yet. But there is a library at the back of the house."

He seemed frustrated, but at that moment, I didn't care. For whatever reason, Moreland was trying to distance himself. I'd had to cultivate that particular skill myself to dissuade gentlemen who were trying to get too friendly. I recognized the maneuver when I saw it. Gone was the man who'd sat next to me and leaned in closely, making me believe he wanted to kiss me. In his stead stood a formal stranger.

I waved a hand toward the back of the house.

"The dining room is next to the drawing room. Feel free to use the library if there's no study downstairs."

He inclined his head, and I took that small motion for the dismissal it was. Turning, I kept my back ramrod straight as I made my way upstairs. I could feel his eyes on me, but I wouldn't turn around. If he thought I was a silly chit who was spinning all manner of *romantic nonsense* because he deigned to smile at me, then he was sadly mistaken.

I was used to men seeing me as an asset, something to be acquired, or as a chore, someone to endure. I refused to behave like the senseless cliché he no doubt thought me to be.

I walked to my room, closed the door, and took in the space. It was well-appointed and clearly meant for a woman, decorated in pale blues with gold accents on the furniture. A richly brocaded gold-white-and-ivory counterpane covered the bed. I wondered, for the first time, if Rexford had ever kept a mistress here. Did he have a mistress now?

It didn't really matter. All I cared about was the fact that Moreland had never had a mistress. It was foolish, but the knowledge made me feel lighter.

I made my way to the bed and sat. What was I supposed to do now?

CHAPTER 11

MORELAND

I watched Victoria climb the stairs, powerless to look away. I was used to getting what I wanted. If she were anyone else, I would have tried to seduce her.

I made my way down the hall to the library, which would suffice for the task at hand. I hadn't been completely honest about needing to compose correspondence. The only people expecting to see me today would make their way to King's, and they all knew about my current responsibilities.

No, what I desperately needed right now was to hide from Victoria. I knew some would call the instinct cowardly, but I chose to consider it a strategic retreat.

Closing the door behind me, I surveyed the library. It was a nicely sized room, its walls lined with mahogany bookcases and a cozy sitting area before a large window. Just to one side was a large desk made of the same wood as the shelves.

To my surprise, the shelves were filled with books, and I couldn't help but wonder if Rexford had purchased the house for himself. He lived above the club and hadn't mentioned that he was considering moving to another residence.

The house was close to his father's ducal manse in Berkeley Square. If Rexford did take up residence here, it would drive Sherbourne to distraction knowing his son lived so close but remained beyond his reach.

Watching the old man's antics amused me. Like clockwork, Rexford's father would send him a summons on Rexford's birthday, expecting his heir to come back to him on bended knee. And when Rexford ignored his summons, Sherbourne would deign to make an appearance in person.

I couldn't remember what we'd been doing the last time he'd arrived, just that we'd been in the billiard room talking about something or other.

When Sherbourne made his appearance, I witnessed firsthand the way Rexford transformed from a powerful, capable man who was admired by many into the wastrel his father thought him to be. He adopted an air of insouciance that enraged the duke. The old man's jowls shook as he clenched his jaw and inclined his head toward the stairs leading to Rexford's study, making it clear that he expected his son to obey. Rexford did, but he never spoke about what happened behind those closed doors.

Ten minutes later, Sherbourne stormed out. When Rexford reappeared shortly afterward, he acted as though the incident had never taken place. I took my cue and never asked him about it. I'd long since accepted the fact that Rexford was a man of secrets.

I made my way to the large mahogany desk and settled into the surprisingly comfortable chair. The surface was bare, but I found parchment, quills, and ink in the top drawer. Pushing aside thoughts of the young woman who was supposed to be my mistress, but whom I could never touch, I composed a note to my steward.

After finishing the note, I dispatched a footman to deliver it. Then I stood and began to pace. My steward would be overjoyed to receive my note.

He'd been trying to get me to go over the accounts for my estates. Since I had a few hours ahead of me, I might as well perform the task I'd been avoiding for some time.

I tried to banish the guilt I felt for avoiding Victoria, remembering the way her eyes had widened with fear when she'd spoken of the gossip column. Her lower lip had trembled, and I'd wanted nothing more than to pull her into my arms. I was no stranger to desire, but I'd never cared about the women I spent time with. We gave each other pleasure, then went our separate ways.

That wasn't the case with Victoria, who I wanted to protect. And no matter how much I tried to convince myself that it was because she was Rexford's sister, I couldn't deny that my feelings for her went beyond duty to her brother. I wanted to take care of her, to watch over her, and to ensure no one ever hurt her.

The hours crawled by, but at least I managed to fill them productively.

When a footman knocked on the library door and informed me that dinner would be ready soon, I nodded my acceptance, grateful for the excuse to escape my self-imposed exile.

CHAPTER 12

VICTORIA

$\mathcal{I}$ was used to being ignored. In fact, I'd relished the illusion of freedom I had when Father left me to my own devices. He made sure I had all the proper tutors and that my spare time was spent in pursuits he considered suitable for a young woman of my station. I knew the staff reported back to him because if I tried to avoid my daily practice at the pianoforte, I would hear about it from Father.

Whenever he was home, Father insisted we have our evening meal together. Those dinners consisted of interminable silences punctuated by questions about what new music I'd learned, what songs I was singing, and whether I thought my skills were sufficient to attract the right suitor. In the end, it hadn't mattered, because he'd arranged my betrothal to one of his cronies without me having to perform one musical recital.

Still, it galled me that on my first full day of freedom, I found myself wandering into the music room and submitting to my daily practice. I blamed Moreland, of course. His presence in the house had my emotions in turmoil. At least concentrating on the music distracted me from wondering what he was doing.

I'd ventured to ask Lily if he required anything, and she'd informed me that he'd sent one of the footmen to his townhouse to fetch some accounts to review, which left me nothing to do but wonder if he found me a burden.

My fingers crashed down on the keys, the discordant notes a fitting accompaniment for my emotions. No matter how hard I tried, I couldn't forget that he was just downstairs—and that he was going out of his way to ignore me.

I stilled when I realized something in the air had shifted. Moreland was watching me. I didn't know how I knew, but I was certain he was there, observing me play, and he'd been doing so for some time.

I placed my hands in my lap, embarrassed by the abrupt ending to my practice session, and shifted on the bench to look over my shoulder. Moreland leaned against the doorframe, his arms casually crossed and his expression neutral.

"I hope I didn't interrupt." He straightened, moving into the room. "I was informed it's almost time for dinner. When I heard the music, I thought that perhaps you might be distracted, so I came to fetch you."

I let out a soft sigh. "If I'd known I had an audience, I would have finished the piece."

Moreland shrugged. "You were practicing, not performing for me."

"That might be true…"

"There are no spies here who will run off to tell your father you've been naughty."

I remembered the gossip column that I still hadn't seen. "I think we both know that my father is very aware of just how naughty I'm being."

The expression on Moreland's face puzzled me for a moment, then I realized the double meaning behind my innocent words. Heat flooded my cheeks. "Not that I've actually been naughty," I added quickly.

He chuckled. "Does it bother you that he thinks you're my mistress?"

It was a serious question, so I gave it serious consideration. I kept expecting second thoughts to creep in and haunt me, regrets for my rash behavior of late, but I couldn't find even a trace of doubt.

I smiled. "I feel free. It's an odd sensation, which makes my behavior just now even more unsettling."

He closed the distance between us. When I shifted to the edge of the piano bench, he took my unspoken invitation and sat next to me. I was facing the piano, and he was facing the other way, our bodies turned toward one another.

"Your behavior?"

I swept my hand over the keyboard. "Practicing. Father insisted I do it every day."

He frowned. "You don't enjoy it? You play very well."

"It's not that I dislike it," I admitted. "It's just that he was so adamant, which took away much of my enjoyment."

"He likes music?"

I realized that I had no idea whether my father

enjoyed music. He'd never bothered to listen to me practice. "I don't believe so. But I'm sure he liked having a daughter he could show off. In the country, he loved having me perform for visiting guests. And I know he had great plans to host a musicale for Lord Heddington." I shuddered, contemplating the fate I'd only narrowly avoided. "Why am I practicing now? I could be doing anything."

"Perhaps it's just a habit," he said softly. "I can help you find something else."

The sincerity in his expression caused me to lean closer. "I think I'd like that very much."

His eyes searched mine for several seconds. "Tell me, Victoria. If you could be doing anything other than practicing at the pianoforte, what would you be doing right now?"

"Not singing." I shuddered. "I am passable at best, but Father insisted I sing on occasion. I hated it. All those eyes watching me, the smirks when I failed to hit a high note." I shook my head. "And of course, he always chose the most difficult songs for me to perform."

His eyes twinkled. "So, you wouldn't want to perform a duet with me right now?"

I laughed. "Certainly not. What I really love to do is draw."

I thought back to the drawing supplies hidden away in my room. Lily knew about them, of course, but she'd kept my secret. The Duke of Sherbourne thought that drawing wasn't an appropriate pursuit for a young woman—an opinion he'd formed when my male drawing instructor began to show me a little too much attention. It was ridiculous because the middle-aged man's interest in me had lain solely with my drawing skills. But of course, Father had assumed the worst and had him banished from the house. Father had refused to hear another word about drawing or painting after that.

Moreland frowned. "Would you like me to sit for you?"

I laughed at the look of horror on his face. "Do you ever sit still?"

"Not if I can help it." He shrugged.

"It must be so tedious for you, being here with me," I teased.

He leaned back. "My steward will be pleased that I was able to go over the accounts. It's a task I tend to put off for as long as possible."

"And now you're going to leave me."

I meant to keep my tone light, but I couldn't hide my sadness at the thought. It was strange that I'd wanted my freedom so badly, yet I was afraid to be alone. A part of my mind whispered it wasn't the solitude I feared, but rather that Moreland fascinated me and I wanted to get to know him better.

I pushed those thoughts away. Moreland was my pretend protector. The world would come to believe we were lovers, but I had to content myself with small moments like this, our conversations drifting toward intimacy but never crossing the line.

"I had to leave all my art supplies at home," I said. "I only brought a small bag. Lily thought to pack for me beforehand, but we took just a few essential items."

Moreland looked as though he wanted to say something, but a footman stepped into the room then.

"Dinner will be served in a few minutes," he announced.

I thanked him and stood.

Moreland did so as well, acting the proper gentleman we both knew he wasn't. He held out his arm for me. "Allow me to escort you to dinner, my lady."

I dipped into a brief curtsy and smiled. "I would be honored, my lord."

Moreland's words and the way he smiled down

at me when I took his arm did much to settle my earlier annoyance with myself.

We made our way downstairs to the modestly sized dining room. Instead of moving aside to allow the footman stationed just inside the room to pull out my chair, Moreland performed the task himself. I couldn't help but wonder if that was something men did for their paramours. Or their wives, for that matter. My mother had died when I was only six years old, so I couldn't recall if Father had ever done the same for her.

The thought was so ridiculous that I couldn't help chuckling. I already knew the answer to that question. The Duke of Sherbourne would never lower himself to pull out a chair for his duchess. He would expect one of the servants to do it.

"Is something amusing?" Moreland asked.

I smiled at him, my mood much lighter in his presence. It was interesting, the effect this man had on me. Only one other man had ever made me feel so comfortable, and that was my brother.

"I was just trying to imagine my father pulling out a chair for my mother."

Moreland laughed. "I doubt he pulls out his own chairs."

I burst into a fit of giggles. "Father isn't quite that bad, but you do paint an amusing picture."

Our first plate was served then, a simple white soup, and we fell into amiable conversation. Mostly, Moreland asked questions about me and my interests.

My life hadn't been all that bad. Yes, my father was strict, but for the most part, he left me alone if I did what was expected. And I'd been able to carve out small moments for myself with my drawing.

When Lily had arrived two years ago to act as my new maid, she'd managed to make things easier for me. I suspected Rexford had arranged for the older woman who'd been serving me before then to retire. She'd been terrified of my father and would never have allowed me to keep art supplies in my bedroom after he'd dictated that I needed to give up my drawing. But Lily had been my ally from the start.

When the meal drew to a close and the footman removed the dessert plates, our easy conversation drew to a halt.

For the first time, it occurred to me to wonder if Moreland had another paramour. He'd told me that he'd never kept a mistress, but I knew he had lovers.

The thought left a sour taste in my mouth. It

was foolish, but in the short time I'd known him, I'd come to think of him as mine. It was the height of folly. After all, he was a Legend. The gossip columns were filled with stories about their love affairs and about the men who gambled with them and lost.

I stood, and Moreland did the same. I could feel the weight of his gaze on me.

"I'm going to—"

We started speaking at the same time and stopped. He inclined his head, allowing me to go first.

"I wanted to thank you for spending the day here. For letting me know about the article and for being so understanding when I overreacted."

He frowned. "It wasn't an overreaction. Your father is used to getting what he wants. You had every reason to worry."

Moreland didn't sugarcoat things for me, which I appreciated. "Still, I don't want to keep you if you have other plans for tonight."

He shook his head. "I have nowhere else I need to be. Everyone knows I'm staying here tonight."

I tried to ignore the way my heart fluttered. "Everyone?"

"Your brother and our friends. Anyone who

happens to be watching this house, both friend and foe."

He was suggesting that my father already knew I was here. I couldn't hold back my shudder of fear at the thought.

Moreland moved to my side and took my hand in his. "You're safe. Even if I weren't here, I happen to know that your brother has his own people watching the house from outside. No one will get close to you."

I took a deep breath and tried to push back my terror. Rexford was very resourceful. He'd somehow managed to outsmart our father, escaping the shackles that the Duke of Sherbourne had spent his life placing around his heir. I'd never asked how Rexford had managed to escape, but he was untouchable now. I could take comfort in the fact that I was under his protection.

"I can't help but think that I'm keeping you from other, more important things."

Moreland raised my hand to his lips, his breath warming the sensitive skin of my inner wrist. "There is no other place I'd rather be tonight." Then he pressed a soft kiss there.

It was a fanciful thought, but my heart stuttered.

He squeezed my hand, then released it. "Go to

sleep, Victoria. I'll be here in the morning when you wake."

I nodded, all words escaping me. I did have the presence of mind to dip into a brief curtsy before turning and leaving the room.

When I reached the stairs, I ran up them, knowing he had probably noticed that my cheeks were burning. I needed to remind myself that Moreland was used to charming women. I meant nothing to him.

But tonight, I would dream of those gray eyes staring down at me and imagine what it might have been like if he'd drawn me into his arms instead of wishing me good night.

CHAPTER 13

MORELAND

I waited for Victoria to leave the room before sinking into a chair. The hovering footmen seemed confused, but I told them to proceed with the task of clearing the remnants of our meal.

I was more than a little unsettled to realize I'd thoroughly enjoyed the meal. Before tonight, every dinner I'd shared with a woman had been a prelude to bedding her. I couldn't deny that I wanted the same from Victoria, but I wouldn't allow myself to take advantage of her when she was so clearly distressed from the unexpected turn her life had taken.

I'd learned a fair bit about Victoria. Until recently, she'd been a dutiful daughter, but she also possessed a determination that shouldn't have come as a surprise. She was Rexford's sister, after all. No doubt a fair bit of that trait came from her father. The Duke of Sherbourne was widely known for his persistence in getting what he wanted.

But Victoria was also compassionate. She'd surprised me when she expressed concern for my safety, and I realized she would willingly sacrifice herself to save me. I was determined to ensure that never happened. Her intelligence and caring nature would be smothered by Heddington. I couldn't stomach the thought of all the things he would do to her once she became his wife.

Victoria had captured my interest the moment I saw her. Any other man in my position—Fairfax, for one—would have wasted no time in wooing her to their bed. With her dark hair, wide blue eyes shining from a face that was almost ethereal, no one would blame me for doing the same. Rexford hadn't forbidden me from pursuing Victoria, but something held me back.

Her innocence was a large part of my reticence.

She was a decade younger than I, but those ten years might as well have been a hundred in terms of our experience. I couldn't help but feel protective of her, even while I very much wanted to take her to my bed and slake my desire.

But I wouldn't do that to her. Not yet, at any rate. I only hoped that my tenuous grasp on my willpower would hold. I'd almost cast it aside when I'd kissed her wrist. It was a self-indulgent moment. I'd wanted to taste her, and the action had seemed innocent enough. But the way she tilted slightly toward me, her eyes darting to my mouth, told me that she would have allowed me to take her in my arms and kiss her. Once I had Victoria in my arms, though, I wouldn't have been able to stop. I wasn't accustomed to denying my desires. If I saw a woman I wanted, I pursued her.

This entire situation had me on edge. I made my way upstairs to the bedroom a footman told me had been prepared for my stay. I couldn't sleep, of course. How could I with Victoria sleeping just down the hall? I lay there for some time, staring up at the ceiling and wondering if she'd locked her door. I hadn't tested the knob when I'd passed her bedroom, but I'd wanted to.

Finally, I gave in to the inevitable. I wouldn't be

able to sleep until I took care of my frustrated desire. I took myself in hand and allowed myself to fantasize about Victoria opening my bedroom door and crawling into bed with me. Here, in my imagination, she wouldn't be an uncertain innocent.

When my release came, I realized that I was in over my head because it did nothing to lesson my desire for her. I shifted onto my side and tried to force myself to think of something else.

To say my sleep that night was restless would be a vast understatement. I wasn't accustomed to waking so early in the morning, so when my valet entered my bedroom at nine o'clock with a folded note, I immediately knew something was amiss.

"Lord Rexford has asked to speak with you this morning," he said.

I opened the note, fearing the worst, but there was no message of disaster, only a few sentences written in Clarence's hand telling me that Rexford wanted to see me at my earliest convenience— which I knew meant right away.

I dressed quickly and made my way downstairs.

I liked a cup of tea in the morning, even if I didn't have time to eat, so I headed to the dining room. I didn't expect a full spread of food for breakfast, but neither did I expect to see Victoria seated at one end of the table, gazing off into the distance.

At my appearance, she jumped to her feet. "I normally have a tray sent up to my room." Her words tumbled out in a rush. "But I didn't know if you wanted breakfast served here."

Recalling our pleasant evening, I very much wanted to step into the room and wait for the servants to prepare our morning meal. I could imagine all manner of pleasant ways to pass the time while we waited.

I forced thoughts back to the matter at hand. "I received a note from your brother. He wants to speak with me."

Victoria seemed to deflate at my words, wrapping her arms around her waist.

I had an almost overwhelming urge to pull her into my arms. Instead, I clasped my hands behind my back and remained where I stood. "You'll be safe here while I'm gone."

She chewed her plump lower lip, and I nearly groaned in frustration as I wondered how her mouth would feel against mine.

Given her nervousness yesterday after learning about the gossip column, I expected that I would have to reassure her. Instead, she nodded, straightened her shoulders, and dropped her arms to her sides. In that moment, I saw in her the same spine of steel that ran through her brother. And damn if her bravery didn't make me want her more.

"I'm not your wife," she said firmly. "And I'm sure men don't spend all their time with their mistresses. People will expect to see you if we want them to believe I am, indeed, your mistress."

She was right, of course. If I spent all my time here, people would realize I was guarding her and not ruining her. I didn't want to leave, but even if Rexford hadn't summoned me, I needed to be seen. I took my leave and forced myself to turn away from her. I could feel her eyes on me as I made my way to the front door.

My carriage was already waiting, but before climbing in, I turned back to the footman who stood by the townhouse door. "Where would I go if I wanted to purchase drawing supplies?"

CHAPTER 14

REXFORD

Since I'd opened King's, everyone assumed I stayed up all night and didn't wake until the afternoon. That was far from my reality.

Yes, the club didn't strictly have a closing time, but I employed enough men I trusted to ensure it ran smoothly, so I normally retired just after midnight. I cultivated the perception of not going to bed until the sun began to rise with strategic appearances throughout the week.

But the truth was that I enjoyed waking early,

when most of the people who'd been at King's were just heading to bed. It was far more efficient to work when no one was around to interrupt me.

Today was no exception. I sat in my study, going through the reports Clarence had left for me. It was a monthly ritual. In his position as club secretary, Clarence would prepare the accounts for me to review at the start of each month. I never found mistakes, but I indulged the habit. It seemed to bring Clarence some measure of satisfaction, and I owed him more than I could ever repay.

Mr. Henry Clarence had been my father's steward and a reliable presence throughout my childhood. If not for him, I would still be under my father's thumb. Clarence had risked everything to bring me the information that allowed me to secure my freedom. Maintaining the facade that he was merely the club secretary was a small price to pay for his loyalty. In truth, he'd always been more of a father to me than the Duke of Sherbourne.

As I scanned the accounts, the quiet morning passed quickly. I was nearing the end of my review when I heard it—the familiar dull thud of a cane, followed by a heavy footfall. The sound sent a jolt through me, though I quickly masked my reaction. I knew that rhythm well.

The Duke of Sherbourne had arrived.

Setting down my quill, I leaned back in my chair and savored the triumph that surged through me. He'd sent a summons yesterday, demanding I appear at his house in Mayfair for a dressing down. As I always did when he sent his yearly summons on my birthday, I'd ignored it. My father had taught me well enough. Control the ground you stand on, and you control the game.

He flung the door open hard enough that it slammed against the wall, then remained silhouetted in the doorway for several long seconds, fury evident in the tight lines of his face. He'd never been one to conceal his anger, and in that moment, it was clear that he'd never been so enraged.

I leaned back in my chair. "This is an unexpected surprise. What could possibly bring the Duke of Sherbourne here so early in the day?"

He entered the room and stopped when we faced each other across my desk. He didn't take a seat, choosing instead to remain standing as he looked down his nose at me. I leaned further back in my chair, refusing to cede ground. We were in my domain, and I was the one setting the rules.

"You've gone too far this time, Rexford." The words were sharp, clipped.

When I'd been forced to spend time under his roof, he'd rarely referred to me by my name. To him I was simply "my son" or "my heir." Now, I was Rexford. It was an acknowledgment, however grudging, of my independence.

"Please, have a seat, Father. You seem distressed."

His grip tightened on the head of his cane. I'd seen him swing that cane at other men, but he wouldn't catch me unaware. Not that I believed he would attempt to harm me. I was, after all, his only heir.

"I demand that you return Victoria," he spat.

I raised a brow. "My sister has gone missing? How troubling. Why am I only hearing about this now?"

"This isn't a game." His cane struck the floor with a loud crack. "People are starting to talk."

"That doesn't seem right. She's always been such a dutiful daughter. The perfect picture of decorum. What could she possibly have done to stir up gossip?"

Color rose in his cheeks, mottling his ruddy complexion. "She is not of age and is under my authority. You will return her to me."

"And if I don't know where she is?"

His eyes narrowed. "You and I both know that isn't true."

This was getting interesting. I waited.

"I've done what I can to quell the rumors," he continued. "That dreadful rag of a paper—*The Mayfair Chronicle*—has been asking questions, but I've put an end to the rumors. Everyone will soon know that she's returned to the country to care for family. She is such a devoted and selfless daughter, after all." He smirked, clearly pleased with himself.

I crossed my arms and raised a brow. "If Victoria is in the country, I don't see why you're here."

His cane struck the floor again. "You have until the sun sets to return her."

I raised a brow. "After you've spread all those careful lies? It wouldn't be very commendable if she returned so soon."

"I could just as easily craft another story," he sneered. "Perhaps her cousin recovered sooner than expected and Victoria was eager to rejoin society."

"Or," I countered, standing to my full height and forcing him to look up at me, "perhaps she won't return at all."

We stared at each other, the silence between us heavy and charged.

At last, he turned away. "You have until tonight. Then I'll be forced to take matters into my own hands."

He limped from the room, leaning heavily on his cane. I'd always considered Father's cane an affectation, or a weapon he liked to keep close at hand. Now, it seemed necessary. As the sound of his footsteps faded, Clarence stepped into the room and closed the door behind him.

"Did you hear that?" I asked.

He nodded. "What do you want to do?"

I sighed, running a hand through my hair. "We can't do anything without Moreland. He's tied to Victoria now and integral to our plans to keep her away from the duke."

Clarence inclined his head. "He spent the night at the townhouse."

"Of course he did," I muttered. I didn't want to know the details, but I trusted Clarence to keep track of what happened between Moreland and my sister. "Send word that I need to speak to him."

Clarence nodded again and left the room.

Father would stop at nothing to reclaim Victoria. I trusted that he wouldn't harm her, but once he had her back under his roof, he would lock her away to ensure she never escaped again. He wouldn't hurt me either. I was his heir, and he believed I would eventually fall in line. But Moreland was in danger, and I needed to warn him.

CHAPTER 15

VICTORIA

Only an hour had passed since Moreland had left, and I was out of sorts.

I wandered into the music room, and my thoughts returned to what had happened there the previous day. I was still annoyed at myself for falling into the same habits Father had demanded I follow. But what was I supposed to do instead? I couldn't leave the house for fear of running into one of my father's men.

Did he know where I was? I shuddered at the thought. No, it wouldn't be safe to leave the house without an escort.

I wandered downstairs to the library, where Moreland had secluded himself yesterday. I ran my fingers over the volumes on the bookshelf closest to the door. They were similar to the ones in my father's houses—leather-bound, their titles etched in gold foil on the spine. I'd already done a cursory search of the room's contents and hadn't found one novel.

I wrinkled my nose as I examined a title. I had no interest in learning about the stewardship of estates. I picked another book off the shelf, my disdain growing. I couldn't help but wonder if Rexford chose the books himself or if they'd already been here when he purchased the house.

With a soft sigh, I turned and exited the room, making my way upstairs again to my bedroom. Once there, I collapsed onto the bed. This was ridiculous. How could I miss him so much when we were newly acquainted? Hours had passed yesterday between when we'd spoken in the drawing room and when we'd had dinner together. But I'd been comforted just knowing he was in the house with me.

I thought about the other men who'd been with Moreland when I'd arrived at King's. It didn't seem possible that only two days had passed. Moreland had been playing billiards with two men who I assumed were also Legends. I hadn't taken note of them but did remember that one was a dark-haired man and the other fair.

Would I feel the same way if either of those men had been tasked with pretending to be my protector? I tried to remember their features but couldn't. For some reason, Moreland had been the one to catch my attention. Something about the way he'd looked at me had given me pause.

It was similar to the way other men looked at me, but normally, I could ignore their interest, the obvious curiosity in their eyes—both young and old —as they wondered what it would be like to win the Duke of Sherbourne's daughter. I hadn't managed to ignore Moreland, though, and I couldn't understand why.

I didn't know much about men, after all. Father ensured I was properly escorted at all times. It was early in the season, but I'd already attended a few balls. I'd danced with a few young men, and more than a few older men, and hadn't met anyone I'd wished would court me. I certainly hadn't trusted them not to press their advantage if we were to find ourselves alone together.

Moreland was different. For some reason, I trusted him. He made me feel safe.

Now that he was gone, I didn't want to leave my room. If one of my father's men burst into the townhouse and tried to take me, I would hear the scuffle between them and the footmen, many of whom were employed for the express purpose of guarding me. But downstairs, without Moreland present, I couldn't help but worry that I was more in danger of being snatched away.

I was just envisioning that scenario when a soft knock at the bedroom door caused me to start. No one my father sent would knock. I sat up and let out a breath of relief when I heard Lily's voice.

"May I enter? Are you here, my lady?"

When I answered, she opened the door and stood there with a wide smile. I didn't think I'd ever seen her so happy.

"Has something happened? Has Moreland returned?"

She shook her head. "He's not here, but he did send something."

I tilted my head, wondering at her strange mood. "What?"

"A few packages have arrived from the baron. I

had them delivered to the music room. I couldn't think of where else to put them."

I couldn't puzzle out what she was saying. Moreland sent me something that was now in the music room? Surely not another musical instrument —not after our conversation yesterday.

I hurried from my room, my curiosity piqued. When I entered the music room, I stopped, shocked at what I found. Easels and canvases lined one wall. On top of the pianoforte bench sat several sketchbooks. Boxes that had been opened lay scattered around the room, but their contents hadn't been removed.

Confused, I approached to investigate one of the boxes and gasped when I saw what was inside.

Lily smiled. "He's sent you everything you could possibly need to encourage your interest in drawing. Charcoals, pencils, colored pencils—even paints."

I walked to one of the easels and ran my hand along the wooden frame. Next to it on the floor were several blank canvases. I brought my hands to my mouth, unable to believe the wonderful, amazing thing Moreland had done for me. I could draw and paint to my heart's content.

I wrapped my arms around my waist and turned to Lily. "I don't understand."

"Clearly, Baron Moreland has discovered your enjoyment of art."

"I told him yesterday that I missed it, but I never imagined…" My voice trailed off when I saw the knowing look in her eye.

Lily approached a box on the chaise nestled into one corner of the room and started pulling out its contents. "We should create an inventory of what's here, then you can decide where you want to start."

CHAPTER 16

MORELAND

After meeting with Rexford, I returned to the townhouse.

I'd intended to go about my normal activities, namely going to Gentleman Jackson's for a round of boxing. I could certainly use the exercise to work out my physical frustrations. But the information Rexford had shared put an end to those thoughts.

A small corner of my mind whispered that I was lying to myself, that I always planned to return to the townhouse to keep an eye on Victoria. I ignored that voice. The matter was out of my hands so there was no point in dwelling on what might have been.

When I let myself into the townhouse, I was heartened to see the three burly footmen who waited at the entrance. I gave them a curt nod, and they melted away, back to their positions. I'd felt guilty leaving Victoria here alone, but the staff's alertness did much to set my mind at ease.

I wandered through the main floor. When I didn't find her in any of the rooms, I made my way upstairs. I wanted to believe that I wouldn't intrude if she was in her room, but I knew that was a lie. Still, first I made my way to the music room.

What I saw stopped me in the doorway, and I smiled.

It appeared as though the small art supply store I'd visited on my way to King's had exploded in here. Packages and boxes were every-where. My gaze settled on Victoria, who sat on a chaise, her brow furrowed as she concentrated on sketching.

I must have made a small sound because she looked up at me. A smile spread across her face, one that filled me with an unexpected emotion—contentment that I'd been able to do something to make her happy.

"Moreland!" she exclaimed, setting aside her sketchbook and rising to her feet.

I expected her to curtsy, but instead, she flung herself into my arms. I couldn't resist wrapping my arms around her and drawing her into a tight hug. To my disappointment, she pulled back all too soon, and I released her.

"I apologize for my exuberance, but you purchased art supplies for me!"

I shrugged, feeling a little embarrassed by the obvious excess. "I asked the shop owner to send one of each type of art medium they possessed." I glanced around the room at the bounty of supplies. "I didn't realize there would be such a large variety."

In truth, I doubt I would have held back even if I had known. Victoria's happiness in that moment eclipsed everything.

"I thought I'd start with what I already knew… sketching." She made a small circle, taking in the array of items that surrounded us. "I suppose I'll have to decide on a few items and put the rest away. There simply isn't enough room here." She turned back to face me, clasping her hands at her waist. "But I can experiment to my heart's content now, work on my drawing. Perhaps I'll have time to practice drawing people. I'm afraid my skills are quite weak in that area."

An offer to model for her was on the tip of my tongue, but somehow I resisted. I was becoming far too immersed in Victoria Wright's life. I needed to remind myself that this arrangement was temporary. When it was deemed safe, she would move on with her life. I didn't want to imagine what that would involve. Rexford would probably set her up somewhere far away from London and their father's country seat.

Thinking of Rexford brought me back to why I'd returned so soon. "I'm afraid I have more news for you."

Her smile dimmed, and she released a soft sigh. Her whole being seemed to deflate before my eyes, and I hated that, for two days in a row, I'd arrived with bad news for her.

"What's happened now?" she asked.

"I spoke to Rexford. He confirmed that your father is searching for you."

She shook her head. "That isn't exactly news."

"He visited your brother this morning."

She wrapped her arms tighter around herself. "I thought he would issue a summons to my brother, but if he actually went to King's…" A shudder went through her. "He must be very angry."

"He's most definitely displeased," I agreed. "But your brother did learn something important. Your father is making it known that you left London to care for an ill family member."

She dropped her arms and looked away from me. "Of course he did. At the first whispers of speculation, he would have done everything in his power to quash it." She met my gaze again after several seconds. "Which means what we're doing here is pointless." She chewed on her lip. "Does Rexford think I should move to the country?"

"That is an option, of course. But not the only one."

She tilted her head to the side, waiting for me to continue.

"We can move forward with plans to hide you somewhere outside of London. Or…" I hesitated. "We can continue as we started and ensure everyone learns you're my mistress."

She turned away and began to pace. "I don't see how. I'm not about to go out into the streets and proclaim it to everyone. And I can't exactly call on my acquaintances for the purpose of announcing that I'm now a fallen woman. Perhaps that makes me weak, but I can't do that."

I crossed to where she'd stopped at the pianoforte and placed my hands on her upper arms, turning her to face me. "No, of course not. But there's still that ball we discussed. The one held for members of the demimonde. When you're seen…" I trailed off, letting her fill in the rest for herself. "Despite your father's efforts to hide what is happening, word will spread. First among men, but eventually, among women as well. Before long, everyone will hear the gossip."

I could see the wheels turning in her head as she pictured the scenario. I far preferred this option to having her disappear forever. She'd agreed to attend the ball when Rexford had first mentioned it, but I had to ensure she hadn't changed her mind.

"Your father's actions have given you a way to end this. You can leave London with your reputation intact, and Rexford will do everything in his power to keep you safe."

She was shaking her head before I'd finished. "Father will never give up. He will do everything in his power to find me. And once he does, he will force me to marry the man of his choosing. He hasn't given up on Rexford yet. A son can perform many ills, and all will be forgiven when they inherit. But a daughter…" She shook her head again. "No, he will not easily allow me my freedom. I serve only one purpose, and that is to form an alliance for him. The path to freedom lies in sullying my name. Only then will he have no use for me."

I examined the determined young woman standing before me, her chin high. "You're certain?"

When she nodded, I released my grip and took a deep, fortifying breath.

She tilted her head to one side. "What do we do now?"

Never in my life had I expected to utter my next words. "We need to see a modiste so you'll have a gown for the ball."

CHAPTER 17

VICTORIA

*I*n short order, I found myself seated in Moreland's carriage. Apparently, it was now *my* carriage. I couldn't see myself wanting to leave the house on my own, but Moreland informed me I would be safe with the driver. The two footmen who accompanied the carriage were also responsible for ensuring my safety.

Despite his assurances, I knew we were at risk out in the open. I told myself that Father wouldn't cause a scene by attempting a public hijacking and tried to force myself to relax. It helped that More-land was seated across from me.

The curtains at the windows were closed, save for the one on the carriage's door. I leaned back against the cushions so a casual observer wouldn't see me.

With nothing else to look at, I examined Moreland. His arms were folded across his broad chest, his gray eyes dark in the carriage's interior. He watched me with what could only be called intense scrutiny.

I kept my hands clasped loosely on my lap. "I'm not going to change my mind."

One corner of his mouth lifted. "I didn't think you would. You are most definitely Rexford's sister."

I shrugged. "We were raised to be resilient. Of course, Father also wanted us to remain obedient to him. Clearly, he failed there."

Moreland said nothing to that.

I sighed. "It seems such a waste to go shopping for new dresses when I've already ordered so many. My wardrobes at home are filled to bursting."

A gleam entered Moreland's eyes. "I don't think any of the gowns you purchased for your debut in society would suffice for this particular assembly."

My mind blanked momentarily, but then I realized he was right. I wouldn't be attending a proper ball, nor would I need to limit myself to wearing demure, maidenly gowns. I'd always been drawn to the brightly colored gowns that married women could wear. And I'd seen more than a few necklines that were cut quite low.

I glanced down at my modest bosom. "I don't think even the lowest neckline would make my décolletage very appealing."

When I looked up, Moreland was staring at my chest. Heat rushed to my cheeks. I couldn't believe I'd said such a thing aloud. And in front of him, no less.

He cleared his throat, then and looked away. "I'm sure that won't be an issue."

I smiled at the implied compliment. I wasn't well-endowed, but perhaps Moreland didn't care about that.

I winced inwardly at the absurd turn my thoughts had taken. I was his mistress in name only. I knew I was pleasing to the eye, but I also knew that much of my appeal lay in the fact that I was the Duke of Sherbourne's daughter. Many men wanted to align themselves with me for that connection. Moreland, however, would suffer for it.

It struck me then that I was being incredibly selfish. He'd assured me he wasn't concerned about what my father could do to him, but I couldn't help but worry. I started to stand, and in that moment, the carriage swayed.

Moreland reached out to steady me, his hands on my hips. "What are you doing?"

He released me, and I moved to sit next to him. It felt natural being so close to him. Despite our short acquaintance, I was at ease in his presence.

"Father will do everything in his power to ruin you." My voice was low.

He shrugged. "He can try."

"You're in danger, and I'm being selfish. Say the word, and I will put an end to this."

We were both turned slightly on the bench seat, our bodies facing one another.

He reached out to take my hands. "No."

"But—"

He covered my lips with a finger. "Don't worry about me. I can take care of myself. And your brother assures me he posted extra security around us."

He grimaced at that last bit, while relief flooded me.

"You don't approve?"

He leaned back, his arms folded across his chest again, and scowled. "I can take care of myself."

I couldn't help but smile. In that moment, he

resembled a recalcitrant little boy. "Perhaps, but it doesn't hurt to be prudent."

I wanted to say more, but the carriage slowed. A quick glance out the open window showed we were on Bond Street. Even worse, we were drawing to a stop in front of Madame Argent's shop.

I shook my head. "We can't go in there. I came here for my dresses for the season. Everyone of import is dressed by her. What if we're seen?"

He lifted one brow, and I wanted to groan at my own idiocy. Of course, that was the point. I was supposed to be seen. But still, the thought of walking into that dress shop, where people I'd met over the last month might turn their backs on me... It made my stomach turn.

"I don't think I'm ready for such a public display of my ruination," I admitted.

His gaze softened. "The shop is closed today."

"But—"

"The dressmaker keeps special hours for other clientele."

I couldn't stifle my gasp. "Madame Argent clothes the demimonde?"

He shrugged. "Apparently."

My eyes narrowed on him. "Do you take all your female companions here?"

He'd told me that he'd never had a mistress, but the question slipped out before I could examine the impulse. An irrational jealousy had me imagining him escorting a long line of beautiful women here.

His gaze met mine directly. "Why on earth would I need to escort a woman to a dressmaker? And you already know I've never had a mistress."

I had nothing to say to that, but his reassurance eased my concerns. It was an odd reaction since we both knew I wasn't actually his mistress.

"Your brother, with his numerous resources, gave me this information. The timing aligned, so I thought it best to handle the matter right away. The seamstress will need time to sew the garments."

I laughed, unable to help myself. "Please, whatever you do, do not call Madame Argent a seamstress to her face. She might accidentally stab you with her shears."

His eyes lit with merriment. "Thank you for the warning."

Moreland climbed down from the carriage first, then turned to me. "Take the cloak," he instructed, gesturing to the garment I hadn't even noticed he'd placed on the bench beside me.

I was glad for his foresight. It was afternoon now, and the streets were filled with people. If I drew the hood and kept my face down, I could hide my identity from curious onlookers.

After helping me down, he offered his arm. I took a deep breath and peeked up at the building before us. I could do this. If Madame Argent provided her skills to members of the demimonde, then she could be trusted to be discreet.

I slid my hand through his arm and allowed him to lead the way. To my surprise, instead of taking me to the front door of Madame Argent's shop, he turned to the left and knocked on the door of the building next to it.

This building had no signage or glass window on the front. I'd never paid attention to it before.

The door opened, and we were admitted by a young man in his late teens. I recognized him vaguely and recalled hearing that he was Madame Argent's son.

Was this her home? It made sense that she would live close to her shop.

We passed through a small entryway and into another dressmaker's shop, one vastly different from her shop next door. It lacked the refined elegance of her main store and instead was vibrant, bursting with color. Unlike her other store, the display of undergarments was out in the open, mere steps from the entrance. Heat rose to my cheeks when I realized that Moreland would see them as well.

Madame Argent greeted us herself, sweeping into the room from what I assumed was an adjoining door that connected to her main shop.

It made sense that if she catered to two separate groups of clientele, she would want to keep them divided. Separate shops and dedicated business hours for each were sensible. Everyone praised the French modiste for her brilliant yet tasteful designs, but it appeared that her shrewdness extended to her business acumen as well.

Her sharp gaze swept over Moreland. "I'm afraid I haven't had the pleasure." She spoke with a lilting French accent that only added to her striking presence. She was of modest height with jet-black hair. Small lines at the corners of her eyes were the only sign that she was slightly older than I had originally guessed.

"Baron Moreland," he said with a slight bow. "At your service."

She clasped her hands. "A Legend! I never thought to have one of you in my shop." She dipped into a curtsy. "Welcome, monsieur. And who is the woman you have brought to me?"

I had kept my head angled away, but at her

question, I turned to face her fully and pushed back my cloak's hood.

Her eyes widened briefly. "Lady Victoria Wright?" She made a small humming sound in her throat. "I've heard rumblings about you, but I was told today that you'd left town to visit family. Something about a cousin being ill."

I braced myself for the censure in her expression, perhaps even a hint of disgust. But Madame Argent was clearly a woman who'd seen much. After that initial flicker of surprise, her face betrayed no judgment.

"As you can imagine," I said carefully, "my father is doing everything in his power to curb the rumors that have arisen."

Madame Argent gave me a reassuring smile before glancing at Moreland. "I can see why you'd be tempted away from the straight and narrow, *non*?"

I was at a loss for how to reply.

Fortunately, Moreland stepped in. "We are here because Lady Victoria had to leave her home quickly. She finds herself without an appropriate wardrobe. She has a few day dresses but no access to the rest of her wardrobe."

Madame Argent nodded. "I understand. I still

have your measurements." Her gaze flicked quickly to my midsection. "I assume nothing has changed?"

Confused, I opened my mouth to ask what could have changed, but Moreland answered for me. "No, nothing has changed."

"Good," she said crisply. "You understand why I had to ask. If one hopes to hide a small baby bump, your modiste should always be apprised."

Heat rushed to my cheeks as I realized everyone would jump to the same conclusion. When they learned that the rumors of my fall were true, they would assume that Moreland had gotten me with child. Nothing else would explain my sudden fall from grace.

"So, what do you two have in mind?"

Her gaze was on Moreland, but I rushed to answer. "Nothing too different from what you already made for me. The dresses were lovely, by the way. I'm sad I won't be able to wear them, but I can hardly ask my father's staff to send them to me."

Madame Argent tilted her head thoughtfully. "I understand. How many dresses did you have in mind?"

"One ball gown," I said before turning to Moreland.

"As many as are necessary," Moreland said. "Whatever you think is appropriate. She won't be going out in public often, for obvious reasons. But we do have a ball in two days' time to attend."

Madame Argent's eyes gleamed. "I understand."

"The other dresses can come at your leisure, but we need a gown quickly," Moreland said.

Madame Argent walked around me, assessing. "I do keep a few gowns prepared for just such emergencies." She met my gaze. "You would be surprised how many young women find themselves here at the last minute, needing something a little out of the ordinary."

I couldn't help but wonder how often situations like mine occurred, and I wanted to press her for details. But if I expected Madame Argent to keep my secrets, I needed to respect the privacy of her other clients.

"Wait here," she said briskly. "I'll bring out a few gowns that I can easily modify for Lady Victoria." She slipped through the doorway into the adjoining shop.

"This feels so normal," I said softly, overcome with surprise.

Our visit wasn't all that different from my last

trip to Madame Argent's other shop. Of course, that time I'd been properly chaperoned by an older woman Father employed to accompany me. I certainly hadn't been here with a man who was supposed to be my protector.

But Madame Argent's calm, understanding manner had lightened the dread I'd felt since the carriage stopped in front of her shop.

Perhaps everything would be fine.

VICTORIA

$\mathcal{B}$efore I knew it, the night of the ball had arrived, and it was time for me to prepare. As Lily performed her magic, I stared at my reflection in the mirror. It was a daily ritual since she'd become my maid. She'd proven adept at creating elaborate yet tasteful coiffures. So, it was a shock when Lily stepped back and informed me she was done.

I frowned at my reflection. "But my hair is still down."

Lily smiled. "It is *artfully undone*."

"What does that mean?"

Her smile was indulgent, as though she knew what was expected better than I did—which, frankly, I didn't doubt. She was only a few years older than I was, yet she carried herself with the confidence of someone who'd seen and experienced far more.

"I started pinning it up here," she explained, gesturing to sections near my temples. "Fortunately, your hair has a natural curl to it, so I didn't have to do much. The way it falls at the back gives the impression that someone—Lord Moreland in this case—ran his hands through your hair while in the heat of passion and started unpinning it."

I stared at her, appalled. "And I'm supposed to let people see me like this?"

Her grin widened, her amusement evident. "Trust me. When you see how everyone else is dressed tonight, you'll think this hairstyle modest."

I was alarmed by her assertion but decided to take her at her word since I knew nothing about the manner of ball I was about to attend.

She dabbed a small amount of color onto my lips. Not enough to look garish, but it did darken my natural hue.

She nodded, pleased with her efforts. "When

you're in the carriage, pinch your cheeks. That'll add to the effect."

I didn't want to know what "effect" she was referring to, so I simply nodded.

She moved to the wardrobe and fetched the gown that had been delivered earlier. It was almost midnight, and I'd been told the ball wouldn't truly begin until the stroke of twelve. I'd caught a brief glimpse of the gown when it arrived, but now, as she laid it out for me on the bed, I was struck by how immodest it was.

"Step out of your chemise," Lily said briskly.

I did as she instructed. She'd seen me without clothing often enough, so I wasn't shy. When she produced another chemise—a shorter, almost sheer one—I tilted my head to one side.

"Why the change?"

She answered with an enigmatic tightening of her lips as she helped me step into it. It barely reached the top of my thighs, and it didn't even cover my breasts.

My mouth dropped open. "Where's the rest of it?"

Lily laughed as she brought out a half corset. "Be patient." She wrapped the corset around my waist and began to lace it.

"Lean forward," she instructed.

Heat rose to my cheeks as I followed the command, lifting my modestly sized breasts as she further instructed. She tightened the laces behind me, and when I straightened again, my mouth fell open in shock.

"What kind of sorcery is this?" I murmured, staring at my reflection in the mirror above the dressing table.

The corset had transformed my figure entirely. I now had a décolletage I could only describe as scandalous.

Lily nodded in satisfaction, then helped me into the gown—my *red* gown, which was a color my father never would have allowed me to wear. It wasn't a bright shade, however, but a deeper color. It would draw the eye while still appearing elegant.

The effect was striking. The red contrasted sharply with my pale skin and dark hair and somehow emphasized the touch of color on my lips. But it wasn't just the color that shocked me—the neckline was so low, I feared I might fall out of the dress entirely.

"I don't think I can go out like this," I whispered, turning to Lily in a panic.

Lily studied me for a moment, her expression

filled with understanding. "You can change your mind," she said softly. "We're not here to force you to do anything against your will."

Her words grounded me. She was correct, of course. This was my choice.

I nodded, resolving to follow through with our plan. It was the only way to gain my freedom. "I'm ready."

There was a knowing gleam in Lily's eyes. "Did his lordship see the dress when you visited Madame Argent?"

I shook my head. "She made him wait in another room."

Her smile widened. "I think he'll be pleased."

When I descended the stairs and entered the drawing room, Moreland was already standing, his hands clasped behind his back. His eyes widened, and his gaze swept over me, taking in the details of my dress. Then he cursed under his breath.

Alarm filled me. "Should I go back upstairs and change into something else?" I knew the dress was a bit much, but Lily had convinced me that he would like it.

He shook his head. "You're perfect. Too perfect, in fact. I'll have a devil of a time making sure no one tries to steal you away tonight."

I shouldn't have been flattered by his words, but I would be lying if I said they didn't send a thrill through me. Moreland thought I was beautiful. Others had said as much, but his appreciation meant so much more to me. And if he was concerned about keeping me by his side, I had no reason to fear his head would be turned by another woman at the ball.

"Should we set off now, my lord? Or is it still too early?"

He glanced at the clock. "It's just before midnight now. We'll have the carriage drive around for a bit since we don't want to appear too eager. Besides, when you make your grand entrance, we want an audience."

I nodded, uncertain how to respond. I took his arm, and he led me outside to the carriage.

Once we were settled inside and on our way, I whispered, "I'm afraid."

He leaned forward and took my hands in his. "This is new to you. To be honest, I admire your courage."

His eyes held mine, and I couldn't look away.

"I don't feel very courageous."

"You will." He reached into a pocket to withdraw something and held it out to me. "This is for you."

It was a mask, made from the same rich red fabric as my gown. I reached for it, and a shiver went through me when my fingers brushed against his palm. Neither of us was wearing gloves.

"Madame Argent sent it along. She said it would match the dress. I wasn't sure I wanted to believe her." He shook his head. "Every eye at the assembly will be on you."

CHAPTER 19

MORELAND

It wasn't my first time attending such a ball. Normally, I was alone when I arrived, which had always suited me. But tonight, as the carriage drew to a stop, I was arriving with my mistress, my very beautiful mistress whom I couldn't touch because she was Rexford's sister.

When we crossed the threshold into the large assembly room, I heard the whispers.

The fact that I was arriving with a companion was surprising in and of itself. I'd never had a mistress, and everyone knew that I preferred to avoid such entanglements—which meant that they were trying to figure out who the woman on my arm could be.

No doubt much of the whispering centered on the gossip column they'd read, the one that said a Legend had taken a duke's daughter as his mistress. But I knew their speculation wasn't about me. No, their interest centered squarely around Victoria. Even without the rumor in the *Chronicle*, she was beautiful enough to draw every eye.

I tucked her more closely against my side as we moved along the perimeter of the room.

Rexford had informed me that he would rally the troops for tonight's event. Hopefully, their presence would be enough to keep Victoria safe. Sherbourne would never think of looking for her here. By the time word reached him, and I had no doubt it would, she would be safely tucked away in Rexford's townhouse again.

I glanced down at Victoria and watched the way her eyes flitted around the large assembly room behind her mask, trying to take in everything. Her movements were slow, her bearing regal, and to the casual observer, she would appear composed. But I could see the cracks in her facade. She was nervous.

To our left, a man led a woman into one of the many alcoves tucked away along the hall's perimeter. He was already pulling down her bodice when she languidly reached up to draw the curtain closed. The way Victoria stiffened against me made it clear she'd seen it as well.

I leaned down to murmur in her ear. Anyone watching us would think I was dropping a kiss on her cheek.

"If you want to leave, just say the word."

She smiled up at me, her wide eyes filled with relief. The force of her gaze hit me somewhere in the center of my chest.

"I believe," she said, her voice steady, "this evening will be quite educational."

My chuckle was unexpected. Damn, but I was really growing to like Victoria.

People made their way to the center of the room. There would be no country dances here. No formal bowing or curtsying as couples faced each other across a respectable distance, only to come together with the touch of gloved hands. Tonight was all about the waltz.

I bowed before Victoria and brought her hand to my lips. "Tell me, my dear, that you know how to waltz."

"I do, my lord." Her lips quirked. "Though I don't think what's happening on the dance floor could rightly be called a waltz."

I grinned as I pulled her into my arms. We started at a proper distance, but when I saw the way people watched us, I knew we would have to put on a show.

"Please forgive me." I placed one palm squarely in the center of her back and pulled her into me. A thrill of awareness speared through me at the feel of her body against mine.

Her mouth dropped open in surprise, but she recovered quickly. "There is nothing to forgive. I am supposed to be your mistress, after all. It's only fitting that I act the part."

She slid her hands up my arms, then wrapped them around my neck. My thoughts stuttered to a standstill.

Her eyes were on me, half lidded and slumberous. The way her hair tumbled about her shoulders made it look as though she'd just risen from bed. The color on her cheeks and lips had my body reacting as though she'd just issued the most licentious of invitations.

She pressed her cheek against my chest, and I took several deep breaths to rein in my lust. I didn't know how I would keep myself from dragging her into one of those alcoves and ravishing her.

Was Rexford already here, witnessing our behavior? That thought didn't summon the guilt it should have. Rexford knew what would need to happen when we'd discussed that I bring Victoria here.

I lowered my head to murmur in her ear. The silky curls of her dark hair brushed my cheek, causing me to close my eyes briefly. "We don't have to stay long. We can pretend we're so enamored with each other that we can't wait to be alone."

She made a small sound, but I couldn't decipher its meaning. I didn't have to. I'd given her a means of escape. It was up to her what we did next.

We spent the next few minutes like that— pressed closely together, swaying against one another. I was acutely aware of the way her breasts flattened against my chest and couldn't help thinking about how they would feel when she was stripped bare.

I kept my hands on her waist, but my thoughts were filled with how much I wanted to grasp her hips and press her into my growing erection. Being so close to Victoria had brought out my baser instincts, and I was powerless to hold them back. If she noticed or was even aware of my predicament, she said nothing.

Finally, after several minutes of delicious torture, I dropped a kiss onto her curls. "We should make the rounds, ensure we're seen."

She pulled back and stared up at me, her eyes blinking open behind her mask. I ground my teeth at what I imagined was heat reflected in their depths. If she felt even a fraction of the desire consuming me, it would be impossible to ensure she kept her innocence.

I tucked her into my side again, and we resumed our stroll. We didn't have to go far before Fairfax and Kendrick approached. They greeted us with a bow of their heads.

Kendrick smiled at Victoria. "It's a pleasure to see you here."

"And looking even more enticing than the last time we met," Fairfax added.

I wanted to punch him. It was irrational since he was only speaking the truth. Madame Argent had done an impeccable job of ensuring every eye would be on Victoria.

She inclined her head. "Are all the Legends here tonight?"

Kendrick nodded and tilted his head to the left. I turned to find Rexford standing against a wall.

Greyson and Clifton stood next to him. All three watched us. I looked away, refusing to feel remorse for my behavior or emotions. Any other man in my place already would have tried to lure Victoria into their bed. Honestly, Rexford should give me a medal.

"Mirabelle is here," Kendrick said.

I nodded. "Of course she is. You're no longer her protector, so it stands to reason she would be looking for another."

"She's hoping one of us will step in," Kendrick continued.

One of us. He meant one of the Legends. She would have to try her luck with the others because I wasn't interested.

"Fairfax?" I turned to him.

He shuddered. "I don't wish to see an article about our upcoming nuptials, thank you very much. If I do take a mistress, it will be someone without such unreasonable expectations."

"She expected you to marry her?" Victoria asked.

Kendrick lifted one shoulder. "It's not unheard of, though it rarely happens. I think she overestimated her charms."

Victoria shook her head. "Perhaps you should

introduce us. She could give me some advice on how to behave like a proper mistress."

"Absolutely not," I said.

Kendrick shrugged again. "It might not be such a bad idea. She definitely knows what she's about."

I scowled at him as he and Fairfax took their leave and faded into the crowd.

And of course, the next person to approach was Mirabelle herself.

CHAPTER 20

VICTORIA

On the surface, this ball was very similar to others I'd attended since my debut. Men dressed in their customary finery, and women went out of their way to dress in a manner they hoped would catch the attention of the opposite sex. But that was where the similarities ended.

The women showed more skin than I was accustomed to. Yes, I'd seen a few women who'd worn gowns with a very daring décolletage, but tonight, that description applied to every woman. Some wore almost sheer white dresses that made it clear they weren't wearing chemises. I'd even spotted a few who had forgone their corsets. The way the fabric clung to their bodies shocked me.

A number of women had gone so far as to wear gowns that, when they moved in a certain way, revealed a slit cut scandalously high along one thigh. If any of the dresses had slits along the front, I sincerely hoped I wouldn't see it. My training in keeping my composure was certainly being tested tonight.

I never imagined I would find myself in the middle of a dance floor, pressed fully against a member of the opposite sex as we swayed together in place. But the way Moreland's arms felt wrapped around me had made me feel secure. It hadn't been a conscious thought to lay my head on his chest. It had felt natural.

The strong thrum of his heartbeat was oddly soothing. As though nothing could happen to me while he was near. But I couldn't deny I'd been embarrassed to realize Rexford had witnessed me draping myself against the baron.

When Moreland's friends moved away, I turned to ask him a question. But whatever it was completely escaped me as a beautiful woman approached us. Her fair hair was voluminous, falling down to the small of her back, and I could tell she was a few years older than me. Her cheeks had lost that roundness mine still possessed. Her face had matured into a perfect canvas for her wide mouth and high cheekbones. The pale blue of her eyes held a hint of amusement.

"My lord." She dipped into an exaggerated curtsy that allowed both Moreland and me to see down the front of her white gown. Of course, she wore a dress that clung to her curves, hugging her breasts and rounded hips. "I didn't expect to see you here with a guest."

Moreland made a small sound, one the woman somehow knew meant he was annoyed.

I couldn't help but wonder why. Was this woman one of his past lovers? Panic threatened to consume me at the thought. If she was the type of woman Moreland normally entertained, I had no hope of capturing his interest.

Clearly, our dance had muddled my thoughts. Moreland was only with me as a favor to my brother.

"Victoria, I would like you to meet Mirabelle Devereux," Moreland said. "Mirabelle, this is my guest, Lady Victoria Wright."

Mirabelle. Lord Kendrick had just said his former mistress was named Mirabelle. My spirits lifted at the knowledge that she wasn't one of Moreland's former paramours. He'd said outright that he had no interest in spending time with her.

Mirabelle's eyes widened, then she laughed. "Does the marquess know you're here with his sister?" She shook her head, her smile indulgent. "I must admit, when I first heard the rumors, I was certain people were lying. But I see you've moved on to corrupting proper young ladies now."

Her gaze swept up and down my body, and heat rose to my cheeks. Given that the woman was a member of the demimonde, I shouldn't be embarrassed. Who was she to judge me?

Moreland did something I never expected. He wrapped his arm around my waist and pulled me to his side.

Mirabelle shook her head and sighed dramatically. "I might have been wasting my time with Kendrick. I never imagined you'd be so brazen as to take Rexford's sister as your mistress. I don't know how you managed it, but I must say that I'm more than a little intrigued."

Moreland shrugged. "Sometimes we are powerless against our desires."

Mirabelle licked her lips, her gaze moving between us. "Perhaps the three of us…"

Her words trailed off, and I couldn't understand what she was implying. But it was impossible to miss the way her hand lingered on Moreland's arm as she leaned in close. I suppressed the desire to throw myself between them.

Instead, I placed a hand on Moreland's chest and met Mirabelle's gaze. "I don't share."

She released her grip on his arm and laughed, her eyes sparkling. I wondered if my eyes ever sparkled but quickly dismissed the thought.

Mirabelle leaned closer and lowered her voice. "You two are putting on a very good show, but if you want people to believe she's your mistress, you'll need to do something scandalous together. That waltz wasn't enough."

She reached into her bodice, pulled out a calling card, and handed it to me. "If you ever want a few pointers, you can contact me. I'll be more than happy to help." She kissed her fingers and waved them in the air as she sauntered away, hips swaying with every step.

Moreland turned us away from the crowd that still watched us. "If Mirabelle has guessed what we're about…"

He didn't need to finish. I understood.

I trailed my hand down his chest until it rested

just above the fall of his trousers. He sucked in a breath and covered my hand with one of his. Then he marched me along the perimeter of the room. He cursed as we slowed at the first, second, and third alcoves. The curtains were drawn, and the muffled sounds from within made it clear they were occupied. Finally, we came upon an empty space, and he led me into it with a lascivious gleam in his eye.

I'd seen that same look on other men's faces when they'd glanced my way, but it had always filled me with revulsion. So, why did I feel... anticipation?

He closed the curtain behind us and released me. We stood there, alone in the darkened alcove, staring at one another. I realized then that I was breathing heavily. So was Moreland.

MORELAND

irabelle's parting words had rattled me. She was more astute than I'd imagined. She'd overplayed her hand with Kendrick, but she could read people. It left me wondering how many others could see that Victoria and I were putting on a show.

Needing time to think, I dragged Victoria into one of the alcoves. But once we were safely away from prying eyes, my thoughts blanked. She was too close. I was supposed to protect her, but somewhere along the way, the pretense had ceased being about helping Rexford. Instead, I was fully focused on the young woman in front of me. And I was very aware of the fact that I was failing her.

She waited for me to speak, but I was powerless to move. Finally, the only thing I could manage was a quick apology as I spun away. I needed to get myself under control.

I didn't expect to feel Victoria's hand on my arm. She wasn't strong enough to move me, but she didn't need to use force. Her light tug had me turning to face her.

Her voice was low. "Miss Devereux knew what we were about. Do you think everyone out there does?"

Somehow I refrained from cursing. "I don't know."

"But you're afraid she might be right."

I nodded. "I've failed you."

Her smile was soft. "There are two of us here, and clearly, neither of us is putting on an adequate show." She looked away, her voice hesitant. "I thought dancing might have been enough."

When her lower lip wobbled, I pulled her into my arms. She took a few deep breaths as she settled into me. Just as she did when we danced.

"If I ever do anything that makes you uncomfortable, let me know, and I will stop."

She looked up at me, her wide, shadowed eyes holding mine. "I think we both know the failing is on my part. Anyone who looks at Miss Devereux knows at a glance that she is what she claims to be —a woman looking for a protector. But with me…" She released a soft sigh that held more than a hint of sadness. "I fear my father has shaped me all too well. I am prim and buttoned-up…" Her mouth twisted to the side, and she glanced down. "A *proper* young woman."

I tilted her chin up so she was looking at me again and allowed my hand to rest there, softly stroking the line of her jaw. "I don't want to hear any negativity from you. We are in this together."

She took a deep, shuddering breath, then nodded. "What are we going to do?"

I stared down at her. "You're still willing to continue? Rexford can take you away. I'm sure he's still out there."

She shook her head. "No, absolutely not. I'm staying with you."

If any other woman had said those words, I would flee. But for some reason, they had the exact opposite effect coming from Victoria. I wanted to drag her home and never let her go. Nothing was stopping me from acting on that desire. I was supposed to be her protector. Her lover. No one in our group would fault me for doing whatever necessary to ensure she was ruined. I closed my eyes for a moment and took a deep breath. I had to find my self-control.

"I think we need to rumple you up a little bit." My eyes roved over her hairstyle. It was already half down.

She blinked in surprise but remained still as I weaved my fingers through the mass and plucked out the few pins that were holding a portion of it up.

I hummed in approval when her hair tumbled down. "That's a good start."

Victoria reached up and pulled at my cravat. I let her. When she had it undone, she pulled aside the opening of my shirt and stared at my throat.

"I've never seen a man's throat before," she admitted softly. "Even when my brother was at home, many years ago, Father insisted that he dress appropriately."

Her words sent a wave of heat coursing through my body. She'd never seen a man's throat. I closed my eyes as images filled my head of all the things I could show her, all the delights we could discover together. I'd vowed that I wouldn't actually ruin her, but at that moment, my restraint was razor-thin. It would take very little to tip me over the edge.

"Can I kiss you?" My voice was unexpectedly rough.

I'd never had to ask a woman's permission before. But my previous lovers had always made it clear that they would welcome my advances. With Victoria, I couldn't be certain.

Her hands moved to my lips, and I captured a finger in my mouth.

Her eyes widened, and she nodded. "I think I would like that very much."

That was all the invitation I needed.

The first touch of our lips was tentative, the fabric of our masks a soft whisper in the darkened space. I could tell she'd never been kissed before. The fact that I was the first man to touch her made me almost wild with the desire to rip the cursed dress from her body. But I needed to remind myself that I had to show restraint. We weren't here for that.

I tried my best to ignore the little voice that whispered, You can do a lot just shy of making love.

She sighed, and when her mouth opened, I deepened the kiss. I kept enough of my wits about me to watch for any sign of reluctance on her part.

But instead of trying to pull away, she wrapped her hands behind my neck, just as she'd done while we were dancing, and lifted herself onto her toes so we were better aligned. I cupped her backside and lifted her against me. She made a soft sound of surprise, but then she returned the kiss with equal fervor.

I didn't know how long we indulged in that simple exploration, but it wasn't long enough. The curtain rattled, followed by a muttered apology, then Victoria and I broke apart.

She was still in my arms, staring up at me, her eyes almost black in the darkness. My baser instincts urged me to finish it and make her mine. She was acting the part of my mistress. Nothing would prohibit us from crossing that final barrier and making it a reality.

We didn't need to pretend.

But then I became all too aware of the laughter and music still playing outside, and for the first time in my life, a wave of shame washed over me. I couldn't do this to Victoria. Not here, at any rate. If we did make love, it wouldn't be here, in an alcove at an assembly. This woman deserved better than that.

I lowered her to her feet and stared down at her

flushed face. Her lips were swollen from our kiss, and it took me a few moments before I found my voice. "I think you might be rumpled enough."

Her laughter held an edge that made it clear she was still trying to gather her wits. Her hands moved to my throat, and I swallowed thickly. Her fingers deftly undid the buttons of my waistcoat, but she paused at the fall of my trousers.

I held my breath in anticipation of her touch. Somehow I forced myself to take another deep breath and covered her hands with mine. "It will be enough."

One thing was clear—I could no longer trust myself to be alone with Victoria. I was as hard as a rock, and I wanted to take her, consequences be damned.

Instead, I tugged her into my side and escorted her from the alcove. Anyone watching us as we made our way to the exit would know we hadn't been conversing in private. And it would only take a glance to see my obvious arousal.

The first clap of a hand on my back as I passed a group of men, accompanied by their bawdy remarks, would normally have been enough to distract me from my desires. But my thoughts were filled with the way Victoria had looked up at me and the way she'd touched me. When she'd hesitated at the fall of my trousers, everything inside me had stilled as I'd waited to see if she would move lower.

I bundled her into the carriage, for which we thankfully didn't have to wait long. Then I had to force myself to remain on the opposite bench from the woman who looked like sin itself. In the dim interior of the carriage, the skin above the very low neckline of her dress seemed to glow in the dark. It beckoned me to touch her.

When she licked her lips, I let out an audible groan. "I shouldn't have brought you here."

Her gaze held mine. "Tell me, my lord, what do you think Lord Heddington would have done to me after we were married?"

Her question lodged in my brain, and I hated the image it called forth. She might be a gently bred young woman, but her father had been on the verge of giving her away to someone who could have done anything they wanted to her.

I'd never given serious consideration to it before meeting her. All those gently bred young women, escorted to all manner of balls, routs, and musicales, carefully protected by their chaperones. Yet many of them were gleefully handed over in marriage to lecherous old men. I had no doubt that most of them were ill prepared for what would happen in the bedroom. The best they could hope for was that it would be quick.

Victoria had escaped that fate, yes, but she wouldn't remain innocent forever. At some point, even if no one would marry her because she'd been thoroughly ruined, she would take a lover.

I could see it all too clearly. She'd told me her plans that first evening over dinner. When this was all over and she was free from her father's control, she wanted to move to a small town, set up her own household, and live quietly. Rexford would help her achieve that goal and ensure she wanted for nothing.

But Victoria was too beautiful to remain alone, and I'd caught a glimpse of the passion that lurked within. Men would flock to her. And it wouldn't matter whether they sought an illicit liaison or offered her an honorable marriage. I hated them all on principle because she was mine.

Somehow, I managed to keep my hands off her during the ride home. I escorted her inside, and a footman assured me that the household had seen no activity in our absence. After dismissing him, I turned to Victoria and inclined my head toward the drawing room. She followed me without protest.

"Do you think it went well tonight? After what Miss Devereux said…" She bit her lower lip.

I laughed. "Trust me, everyone thinks we're lovers."

She let out a shaky breath as she reached up to undo her mask. I'd already removed mine in the carriage. "Because I undid your cravat and the buttons of your waistcoat? Or because my hair was down?"

I shook my head. Lust had me reaching for the hand that wasn't holding the mask and bringing it to my still-hard erection. "No. Because it was clear to everyone that I couldn't get you out of there fast enough. They think I'm bedding you right now."

I expected her to snatch her hand back when I released her. Instead, she curled her fingers around me, and I had to close my eyes. Never in my life had I been so tempted by someone I knew I couldn't have.

"We could still do that." Her voice was low and melodious, a siren's call. "I am your mistress, after all."

Cursing, I dragged her into my arms and ravished her mouth. I poured every ounce of frustration and desire into our kiss, welcoming the way she returned my ardor. Then I pushed her away.

"I know what I want," I said, a low gravel in my voice. "But you need to be certain you want the same thing."

"I do," she whispered.

I shook my head. "No. Not tonight. You should go upstairs now. You'll sleep in your bedroom, and I'll sleep in mine. We can talk about this tomorrow."

She wanted to protest. I could see it in the stubborn tilt of her chin and the way her lips pressed together in that delicious line that tempted me to coax them apart. But after a moment, she nodded.

I watched her walk away, her back ramrod straight, her long, dark hair swaying with every step. And I cursed myself for behaving like a fool.

CHAPTER 22

VICTORIA

I'd become very good at compartmentalizing my feelings, which was the only reason I could go upstairs and prepare for bed. I even managed to fall asleep quickly and dreamed of what could have happened between Moreland and me if he hadn't sent me away.

When morning dawned, I woke early and rang for Lily. Anticipation filled me as I thought about Moreland's last words to me. Today, we would discuss our relationship.

I hadn't changed my mind. Last night had

shown me that I wasn't afraid of experiencing intimacy with him. In fact, the opposite was true. I yearned for his touch.

If I could only have him for a short time, I would accept that. Whatever happened in the bedchamber between us would be preferable to what I would have experienced in my marriage bed with Lord Heddington.

"Is Lord Moreland awake?" I asked as soon as Lily entered my room.

Lily shook her head as she moved to the wardrobe and pulled out a dress. "His lordship was called away early this morning."

My spirits fell, and I crossed the room to the dressing table, where I stared down at the assortment of hairpins and brushes spread over its surface. "Did he leave a note for me?"

She moved into place behind me and began brushing out my hair. "I'm afraid he didn't have time. But he did leave word with the butler that he'd be back in time for dinner."

I let out a soft breath. "You can send a tray up to my room for breakfast. There's no point in putting the staff to a great deal of effort on my behalf."

"As you wish, my lady."

Silence stretched between us as she finished pinning my hair in place and helped me dress. The day yawned before me, but at least I would be able to draw, thanks to Moreland's thoughtful gift.

After Lily left to arrange my breakfast, I settled onto the side of the bed and tried not to worry. But I would be lying if I said I wasn't concerned that Moreland had changed his mind.

He'd likely decided his allegiance to my brother meant he couldn't touch me. He'd said as much before, but I'd hoped the situation had changed after everything we'd done last night. He'd been on the verge of losing control.

I had to figure out how to bring him to that edge again.

My gaze fell on the side table and the calling card I'd placed there last night, Mirabelle Devereux's calling card. When Moreland and I had entered the alcove, I'd followed her lead and tucked it into my bodice. I'd forgotten about it until I was preparing for bed. I reached for it now. Her name was embossed on the front. Turning it over, I saw an address written in fine script. My excitement grew as I considered how she might help me.

I was too embarrassed to ask Lily what she knew about men. But Mirabelle had been Lord Kendrick's mistress. She would know how to entice a man and hold his interest.

I chewed my lower lip, considering my options. I couldn't go see her, but I could invite her here. With a grin, I stood and went in search of a quill and parchment.

IT WAS EARLY AFTERNOON, and I was in the drawing room as I waited for Miss Devereux's call. I was beginning to worry she wouldn't accept my invitation when I heard the knock at the front door. I wasn't sure if it was wise to befriend the woman, but it couldn't hurt to make her an ally.

I stood and waited for the butler to show her in. The soft lilt of her voice preceded her arrival. But the woman who walked into my drawing room bore only a superficial resemblance to the one I'd met last night. Today, I wouldn't have been surprised if someone told me she was a member of the ton. Her fair hair was swept up in a modest arrangement, her face devoid of cosmetics. And her gown was one I could see myself wearing while going on calls of my own.

I was amazed at the difference in her appearance. Last night at the assembly, she'd been the sultry temptress. Today, she was the picture of a proper woman who would know how to comport herself in any situation.

"I'm so pleased you accepted my invitation, Miss Devereux."

She crossed into the room and dipped into a circumspect curtsy. "I was honored to receive your note. And please call me Mirabelle."

We settled onto the settee. "I've already arranged for tea. It should be here shortly."

Mirabelle examined me. "Is this simply a social visit?"

I hesitated, momentarily caught off guard by her forthrightness. I'd made it this far, however, so there was no point in delaying the inevitable. "You said something last night that intrigued me."

Mirabelle's smile turned calculating. "I saw you and Lord Moreland go into the alcove. When you exited, I thought for certain I'd been mistaken in my assumptions."

I tried to ignore the heat rising in my cheeks,

and I lifted one shoulder in what I hoped was a casual shrug. "I have a few questions for you."

She leaned forward. "I must admit my curiosity is piqued."

I took a deep breath and launched into the details I'd decided to share with her. "You know who I am."

She nodded. "You're Rexford's sister, are you not? I wasn't sure I could believe the rumors."

When I nodded, she shook her head. "I still can't believe Moreland took his friend's sister as his mistress. Your father must be furious."

I looked away. "What my father thinks right now hardly matters."

"Tell me," she said. "Why would you choose to be a man's mistress instead of marrying a titled gentleman who could give you everything you want?"

I met her curious gaze. "Because my father wanted me to marry Lord Heddington."

Mirabelle winced. "I see your dilemma."

I nodded in agreement. "This was the better alternative."

"Perhaps," Mirabelle said. "But a man of Lord Heddington's age… He might not have bothered you all that much."

I frowned. "Bothered me?"

She laughed softly. "You are most definitely an innocent. When men reach a certain age, many find themselves unable to perform."

My frown deepened. "Perform?"

She shook her head. "Have marital relations. Bed their wives. They cannot… physically perform the deed. So you might have found you were like a daughter to him. Someone to accompany him to balls and host his gatherings."

I considered her words, wondering if I'd been too hasty. But then I remembered the way Moreland had looked at me last night, how he'd purchased every art supply conceivable because he knew I liked to draw. And I couldn't deny the way my body reacted whenever he touched me. No, I didn't regret what I'd done.

I shook my head. "There's no telling. In all likelihood, the opposite might be true. He doesn't have an heir, after all. I'm sure he's quite anxious to ensure the title passes to a son."

Mirabelle sighed. "You're probably correct. And Moreland is very attractive…" She trailed off, then let out an incredulous huff. "I just can't believe your brother is fine with this."

I raised a brow. "Have you met my brother?"

She laughed. "You have me there. He is widely regarded as the king of the Legends, after all. And their morals are looser than most."

I had no reply for that. Not when Moreland was showing a frustrating amount of restraint when it came to his behavior toward me.

"So, tell me, Lady Victoria. Why did you invite me here today?"

I took a deep breath and forced myself to bare my soul to this woman. "I'm having an issue with Moreland."

She tilted her head. "Please don't tell me he has issues… performing."

"No, of course not," I said quickly, recalling how hard he'd been last night, the way he'd felt under my touch. I had no evidence to the contrary, but I was sure Moreland would have no issues in that department. "It's just… at times, I find it difficult to make him forget I'm Rexford's sister. He's too circumspect around me, and I lack the knowledge in how I can entice him to let go of his restraint."

Mirabelle's gaze sharpened, and I had the uncanny certainty that she'd realized the truth— that Moreland and I hadn't made love yet and that I hoped to tempt him.

"Ah, here is the tea," she said as a footman entered with a tray of tea and sweets. She waited for me to pour us each a cup before continuing. "I have much information to share with you that will be of great benefit."

Relief spread through me. I'd most definitely done the right thing in reaching out to this woman.

VICTORIA

My conversation with Mirabelle was eye-opening. I didn't try to hide the fact that my knowledge had significant gaps. But I couldn't ask the one question about which I was most curious. What would it feel like to have a man push inside me for the first time?

I'd heard whispers about pain, but I was starting to question whether that was true. Especially since Mirabelle made it clear that she enjoyed the act of making love.

If she thought my reluctance to share details about my experiences with Moreland was odd, she kept that to herself. I'd been sheltered, after all, and had just come out in society. I knew that she assumed my reluctance to divulge any details was due to my inexperience.

After she left, my thoughts whirled with possibilities. But I could hardly do some of the things she'd suggested when I still needed to convince Moreland not to push me away.

I spent the rest of the day experimenting with oil paints and quickly discovered I had no talent for them. I would have to continue with watercolors, which I'd only just started using before Father had stopped my art lessons.

When evening approached, I put aside the paints and brushes. Time was running late, and I had to ask one of the maids to clean my brushes. It felt indulgent, but I had to prepare for Moreland's arrival.

I hurried upstairs and summoned Lily to help me into the gown Madame Argent had sent that afternoon. It wasn't one of the more risqué styles she'd suggested, but the fabric had looked lovely against my skin.

I gazed at the dress, which I'd asked Lily to lay out on my bed. It was pale blue, its fabric shimmering in the late-afternoon light that filtered through the window. The bodice was modest yet flattering. It was a gown suited for an evening affair, though perhaps a bit formal for a private dinner at home. Still, I wanted to look my best for Moreland.

I considered asking Lily to take down my hair, but in the end, I shied away from the request. She knew that Moreland and I slept in separate bedchambers, and I couldn't admit that I hoped tonight would put an end to that arrangement.

When I made my way downstairs, I was pleased to discover that Moreland was already waiting for me in the drawing room.

His gaze swept over me, taking in my formal attire. "Were you planning on going out tonight?"

Nervous energy filled me as I closed the space between us. "I don't have many dresses here."

"You always look beautiful, Victoria."

I blushed and moved closer to him, resting a hand on his arm. For a moment, I feared he would push me away. Instead, his expression softened, and he gave me the kiss I'd been hoping for. It was nothing compared to the passionate embrace we'd shared last night, but it signaled that he didn't intend to reject me.

Our kiss was short, and all too soon, he released me. "I was told that you had a guest today."

I sighed. Given my precarious situation, it made sense that the staff would report any comings and goings to him. "I thought that, given my position, it might be worthwhile to speak with her."

He frowned. "You don't need advice from Mirabelle Devereux."

I raised a brow. "Am I not your mistress?"

He swore under his breath. "You won't be moving from protector to protector in a series of short-term arrangements. What we have here..." He shook his head. "I don't even know what I'm saying. I'm not sure what we're doing."

"You know that I admire you and that I find you attractive."

His eyes darkened, his gaze searching mine as I bared my soul.

Terrified that he would change his mind, I continued. "I've been thinking about what happened last night, and you should know that my feelings remain the same."

He smiled then, and the only word to describe it was sinful. "Your brother will call me out for this."

"I doubt that very much. From everything I've heard, he wouldn't be in a position to judge my actions."

"Perhaps not. But I was asked to protect you."

I placed a hand on his arm as concern bloomed in my chest. "Did he warn you not to…?" I trailed off, unable to finish the sentence. How exactly could I phrase this when I was too embarrassed to ask for what I really wanted from him?

He shook his head. "He warned me not to hurt you. But I think he knew that, given the situation and how close we'd need to become…" He shrugged. "I think he realizes that it is inevitable."

"Because you are known for bedding many women." Mirabelle had told me as much, and I hated the images that had sprung to mind. "Have you been seeing anyone when you're not here?" I couldn't keep the question from slipping out. It was my greatest fear that he was playing nursemaid to me while seeking pleasure elsewhere.

"No, Victoria." His voice was firm, steady. "I haven't been able to think about another woman since meeting you."

The dark note in his voice made my stomach tighten. "I'm not sure how I'm going to eat right now."

He laughed then, his expression almost boyish. "I'm sure we'll manage."

CHAPTER 24

MORELAND

She bit her bottom lip, and I wanted to groan. With any other woman, I would think it a practiced move designed to draw attention to her mouth. But with Victoria, I knew it was an indication she was unsure of how to proceed.

"Your butler informed me that dinner would be served when we're ready." I held out my arm, and she took it, sagging against me a little. It was unwise, but affection for this woman bloomed in my chest.

Dinner was enjoyable. I'd never had so many meals with the same woman, but Victoria was filled with amusing stories about her childhood. She didn't remember much about Rexford, given their ten-year age gap and the fact that he'd been away at school for much of the year. And I thought it best not to share the stories I knew about him.

A tense silence settled over the room when a footman took away our dessert plates. I assumed she was worried about what would happen next, and I wanted to assure her that I wouldn't force her to do anything. I would be disappointed if she changed her mind, but I would accept her decision.

I should have known she was still worried about the duke.

"Father was very upset when Rexford started his club." She bit her lip again. "But my brother is his heir, and at some point, Rexford will be forgiven. But with me…" She looked down at the tabletop, which had been cleared. "He'll never forgive me."

"Victoria—"

"I don't expect him to, and I don't need that from him. But I'm frightened of what he'll do when he finds me."

I stood and circled the table to stand beside her. I held out a hand, which she took, and pulled her to her feet.

"Your father won't find you. Rexford has done

everything in his power to ensure we're safe here. You also have me. I promise to keep you safe."

She swallowed visibly, then nodded. "I want to believe you."

I cupped her cheek. "You might not believe me yet, but it's true. And for that reason, I want to let you know that if you've changed your mind about tonight, I will respect your wishes."

Her eyes met mine, and I saw all manner of emotions cross her face. But the predominant one was fear. Disappointment threatened to crush me, but I released her and stepped back.

"No." She reached for my hand again. "I haven't changed my mind. I'm afraid that you'll find me lacking. You have so much experience…"

I pulled her into my arms and kissed her then. I didn't want Victoria to think about the other women I'd been with, because in that moment, no one else mattered. I only wanted her.

It wouldn't last. It never did. But that didn't mean we couldn't enjoy what we had now.

Her kiss was tentative, but then she wrapped her arms around my neck and sank into me. I vowed that I wouldn't take her maidenhead this first night, but nothing could stop me from initiating her into the world of physical delight.

I pulled back, and together we made our way upstairs to her bedroom. No servants lurked in the hallway, but I knew they would be aware of what was happening between Victoria and me. The servants always knew, which meant that Rexford would also know, but he wouldn't have put his sister in my care if he didn't trust me.

I closed the door behind us, then turned to look at Victoria, who clasped her hands at her waist.

"Tell me what you want me to do, my lord."

Those words coming from her delectable mouth had me rock hard, which was an inconvenience.

"Turn around."

She did, dropping her hands to her sides as I moved into place behind her and began undoing the row of buttons along the back of her dress. I dropped a kiss at the base of her neck where it met her shoulder and saw goose bumps rise on her arms.

"Don't be afraid," I said.

She shook her head. "I'm not afraid. I find that I'm looking forward to this."

When I reached the last button, I pulled down her dress. I released it to fall on the floor, then set to work undoing her corset. I threw that onto her dressing table.

"Turn around for me."

She was still in her chemise when she turned and stepped out of the pile of fabric on the floor. A candelabra burned brightly on the night table behind her, allowing me to see the shape of her figure beneath her chemise. She was glorious. My fingers itched as an almost desperate need to rip that flimsy fabric swept over me, but somehow, I held back. Her hand moved to the ribbon that held her chemise together at her breasts. If she stripped for me now, I wouldn't be able to maintain even a modicum of restraint.

I swallowed thickly. "Leave it on."

She let out a breath of relief and moved to lie on the bed. Her hands fisted by her sides, and she gazed up at me.

"Are you going to—"

I shook my head. "I won't bed you tonight, Victoria."

She rose onto her elbows, but I placed a finger on her delightful mouth to stem her protest.

"Not tonight, but I will show you the pleasure to be had when a man touches you."

I waited for her nod. When she lay back again, I allowed myself to touch her. I started with her lips, tracing them with my thumb before settling onto the bed next to her and kissing her. She made a soft, contented sound and turned into me. I traced the line of her jaw, then her throat, following the touch with my lips.

When I cupped her breasts, her gentle moan shot through me. Never before had I devoted myself so completely to bringing pleasure to a woman with no thought of my own release. But in that moment, all I cared about was ensuring Victoria enjoyed my touch.

I swept my tongue over the peak of one nipple, through the chemise, wetting the fabric, then drew the tip of her breast into my mouth. Her hands flew to the back of my head, holding me there as she made low, mewling sounds in the back of her throat. Each whimper served to ratchet up my desire. I moved to lavish attention on her other breast, then kissed my way down her belly.

I met her gaze, needing to prepare her for what was about to happen. "I'm going to touch you between your legs."

She nodded, her plump lower lip held between her teeth. "Yes," she breathed after releasing her lip.

I grinned. She was trying to hold back. I intended to make her scream.

I watched her face as I trailed my hands from

her delicate ankles, along her calves, then up her soft thighs. I stopped just before I reached my destination.

"Have you changed your mind, Victoria?"

She shook her head. "No."

Desire surged through me, knowing what I would find when I reached her core. She was soaking wet. My amusement fled then as I explored her. When I brushed a thumb over that small bundle of nerves, she whimpered. I devoted my efforts there as I slipped one finger inside her. She was biting her lower lip again.

I wanted to bring her to release with my mouth, but that would be too much for her first time. Tonight, I would limit myself to using my hands.

"Scream for me, Victoria."

Her breath hitched, then she did just that. As she tightened around my finger, I continued to stroke her. When the tremors were over and she sagged into the mattress, I stopped and lowered her chemise to cover her.

She was on her elbows again, staring at me, her eyes wide with amazement. "I never—" She shook her head. "No wonder men stray."

I laughed. That was the last thing I'd expected her to say.

"I'm eager to experience what happens next."

I was powerless to stop myself from kissing her. But I couldn't allow myself to linger, so I pulled back. "That is enough for tonight."

She clutched my arm to stop me.

I dropped a kiss on her forehead and smiled. "We will do this slowly or not at all."

Her eyes locked on mine, then she nodded.

"Good." I brushed her hair away from her face, then rose from the bed. Turning, I left the room before I gave in to the overwhelming temptation that was Victoria Wright.

VICTORIA

Mirabelle's invitation arrived near midday the next morning.

Thank you for inviting me to tea yester-day. I have a few appointments scheduled this afternoon. If you're not receiving calls today, I thought you might like to come with me. I would like to introduce you to my modiste.

I'll call at four o'clock unless I hear otherwise.

- M.D.

I stared at the simple note and considered the wisdom of accepting.

After our all-too-brief intimacy yesterday, I'd expected to find Moreland gone this morning. To my delight, he'd been waiting for me in the break-fast room. Unfortunately, after breaking our fast, he took his leave.

Needing to distract myself, I wandered up to the music room. Or more accurately, the room that was now my artist's studio. Cupboards had been moved into the room to store the art supplies, but I loved seeing the easel and canvasses lining one wall. It was a daily reminder that I no longer needed to hide my interests.

I picked up my sketchbook and flipped to the page where I'd tried, without success, to draw Moreland's features. I frowned down at my pitiful effort to capture the gleam in his eyes when I'd first caught sight of him at my brother's club.

I had always thought the marriage bed was an ordeal I would need to tolerate, but Moreland had shown me that didn't have to be the case. Perhaps husbands were dull creatures, but protec-tors were another matter entirely. Given the choice between continuing this ruse with him or marrying Lord Heddington, I would vastly prefer to spend the rest of my days as Moreland's mistress.

It would never happen, of course, but that didn't mean I couldn't enjoy our time together. And perhaps afterward, I could find someone capable of bringing me even a fraction of the pleasure he'd already shown me.

I picked up a pencil and settled onto the chaise, determined to have a picture of Moreland to remember him by. Unfortunately, my second and third sketches weren't much of an improvement. Blowing out a frustrated breath, I put down the sketchbook and glanced at the mantel clock. It was almost time for Mirabelle's visit.

When I returned downstairs, I found myself facing a disapproving butler.

"It is out of the question, my lady."

His tone and demeanor were proper, but he was younger than one would expect for such an exalted position within the household staff. Given that he was assigned primarily to ensure my safety, it made sense that my brother would hire staff composed of younger men, men who could deal with any attempts my father might make to steal me back.

I was determined to hold my ground. "Was that my brother's order? That I cannot leave at all?"

The butler frowned. "Not in so many words, but it was implied."

I raised a brow. "Implied? So you're not following his orders. You're keeping me locked here of your own accord."

"It is extremely unwise for you to leave. We would not be able to protect you."

I smiled sweetly. "Then send an escort—your strongest fighters. We'll take our own carriage, and one of your men can travel in the coach with us. Another can sit outside with the driver. I'm sure that between the three of them, I will be quite safe. I'm only going to visit a modiste. I made a similar visit with Lord Moreland recently." I leaned in slightly. "I would hate to tell my brother that someone on his staff was being unreasonable."

The color drained from his face, and I felt a twinge of guilt.

He nodded stiffly. "Remain here while I arrange for your escort. Miss Devereux needs to leave the address of the modiste with me. And of course, I will send word to Lord Rexford about your outing."

I smiled. "That is acceptable."

Ten minutes later, Mirabelle and I were seated in my carriage, while Mirabelle's carriage followed. In addition to the men accompanying the vehicles, two outriders followed at a distance. The footman who rode with us in the carriage was a burly young man.

"My, my, my," Mirabelle murmured, leaning forward and giving him a seductive smile. "I didn't expect you to come with company." She glanced at me. "Tell me, does Moreland invite him everywhere you two go?"

Color crept up the man's neck, but he said nothing, his expression impassive.

I had no idea what Mirabelle meant. Rather than ask, I thought it best to change the subject. "Moreland just wants me to be safe. As you can imagine, my father isn't happy with our arrangement."

Mirabelle nodded. "I understand. And I'm pleased you accepted my invitation today."

"I must admit that I've been to a modiste since my change in station. Madame Argent."

Mirabelle smiled. "That's all well and good. Madame Argent is very talented. But she's also a bit… conventional." Her eyes glinted with something unreadable. "My modiste can help you in other ways."

She gave me a significant look before her gaze slid to our companion. My breath caught as I recalled some of the nightgowns that had recently been delivered to the townhouse. If Madame Argent was conventional, I was almost afraid to see what Mirabelle's modiste would suggest.

I wanted to ask Mirabelle for more details but couldn't with the footman in the carriage. I wasn't entirely comfortable discussing personal matters in front of men I didn't know well. In truth, I wasn't comfortable discussing such things in front of men at all. Except for Moreland. After the intimacy we'd shared last night, it might be enjoyable to raise the subject with him.

It was difficult to ignore the man seated on the bench opposite us, but I was curious about Mirabelle's current situation. "Moreland mentioned that you're looking for a new protector."

Mirabelle shrugged. "Such is the way of the world when it comes to women like me."

"How are you faring otherwise? If I can do anything to help you, please ask."

I owed her that much at least. She was the only person who'd reached out to befriend me now that I was ruined.

An odd emotion flickered across Mirabelle's face, but it vanished as quickly as it came. "You are very generous, definitely a credit to how you were raised. In another lifetime, I think we could have been friends."

I smiled. "We can be friends now."

Mirabelle leaned closer, lowering her voice. "Are you sure you wouldn't rather return to your father? It's not too late. I can help you if you've changed your mind and come to realize that you're in too deep with your current situation. I'm sure your brother would understand." She seemed so distraught.

I was touched by her concern. "You needn't worry. For the first time in my life, I'm happy."

Her face fell, and I couldn't help but wonder if she was thinking about her own circumstances. Living between protectors and searching for someone to take care of her must be difficult. I imagined she thought that I was insane to give up the security inherent in my former life.

I hated to think that I might someday find myself in a similar situation. Once this uncertainty settled and I was truly free from my father's control, Moreland would tire of me. He'd admitted that he'd never kept a mistress, and undoubtedly I lacked the skill in that department to keep his interest for long. Then I, too, would be alone. But unlike Mirabelle, I had my brother's support. I didn't need to seek another man to take care of me. Rexford would ensure I stayed safe.

"Please don't worry about me." I laid a hand on her arm. "I am quite content." I turned to look out the window when I realized the carriage was slowing. "It appears we've arrived."

Before I could make out where we were, the carriage door flew open. To my shock, Moreland stood in the opening.

"Get out."

I froze. I'd never seen him so angry. But before I could obey, Mirabelle murmured a quick apology and scurried from the carriage. Moments later, Moreland was sitting beside me. The man who'd accompanied Mirabelle and me had departed with her. It was just the two of us inside the carriage. As the vehicle jolted forward once more, I examined Moreland, wondering why he was so angry. I'd taken precautions, after all. But his fury was clear in the tightness of his jaw and the way his fists clenched at his sides.

Had he been my father, I would have been terrified. But I wasn't afraid of Moreland because he wasn't just angry. I'd felt the same emotion too many times myself not to recognize it in another. He was terrified.

CHAPTER 26

MORELAND

I hadn't been able to shake my concern from the moment I'd received word that Victoria had gone out with Mirabelle. But I'd tried to assure myself that she was properly escorted. After all, Mirabelle was harmless.

Then Rexford had come out of his study, and he, too, had received a report. I should have realized that he had men watching his father's house. He'd learned that the duke had left his home, escorted by a veritable army of footmen and thugs. Mirabelle had betrayed Victoria.

Fear slid through my veins at Rexford's grim expression. "Sherbourne left the house an hour ago."

I saw the entire situation play out in my mind. Mirabelle was leading Victoria to where Sherbourne and his men would be lying in wait. I pulled out the note the butler had sent me and tossed it in Rexford's direction before storming from the club. There was no time to waste. I set out on horseback for the small backstreet in London, riding hard, my heart threatening to explode from my chest.

I didn't know what Mirabelle had told Victoria, but it didn't matter. She could say anything, and Victoria would believe her. Victoria was far too trusting. Despite spending her entire life as her father's prisoner, she still liked to see the best in others.

I'd been the recipient of that faith, but now, so had Mirabelle.

Rexford had shouted that he would send men to assist, but I was desperate to get there first.

When I finally reached the street named in the note, I dismounted. Fear that I was too late consumed me. I wanted to storm into the small establishment where Mirabelle was taking Victoria.

Some instinct held me back. I'd come from the club, which was closer than the townhouse, and I'd been on horseback. It would take the carriage longer to reach the shop. If I rushed in and Sherbourne's men were still lying in wait, they would dispatch me quickly. Still, I couldn't help picturing Victoria being forced out the back of the store.

My mind made up, I took a step toward the shop's door. Then a carriage pulled onto the street. It was impossible to be sure, but I thought it looked like Victoria's carriage. I waited, my muscles tense. My gaze swung between the storefront to the approaching carriage. Like Madame Argent's second store, this modiste shop lacked glass windows. A detail that worked in my favor.

I patted my horse's shoulder and loosely tethered the reins before springing into action the moment the carriage came to a halt. My heart still pounded, the fear that had driven me through the streets of London transforming into something else. Anger. Not at Victoria, though. Never at her.

No, my fury burned for Mirabelle and for Sherbourne.

Kendrick's former mistress would be wise to lie low for some time. Because if I saw her again... I shook my head. I wouldn't harm her, but she would never come near Victoria again.

I flung open the carriage door and ordered a startled Mirabelle to leave. The guard who'd been with them wisely decided to exit the carriage as well. I gave him instructions to take care of my horse before turning to Victoria.

The carriage began to move and my heart pounded as I stared at her, emotion swamping my senses. Her lower lip quivered before she caught it between her teeth. She straightened her shoulders and met my gaze.

"I was properly escorted, and I told the butler where we were going." She folded her hands in her lap but didn't look away. "I didn't realize I wasn't allowed to leave the townhouse. I was only going to the modiste. We had a larger escort than when you and I made a similar trip."

I forced myself to take a deep breath, but my heart refused to slow. "Do you know how close you came to falling under your father's control again?"

The color drained from her face. "What?"

"Mirabelle was leading you straight to Sherbourne." My voice was tight, barely containing the anger still churning inside me. "That dressmaker?

Rexford has men following your father. He's waiting in there along with others. I don't think I need to tell you what they planned to do when you entered the shop."

Her face fell. "I didn't know. Mirabelle was so nice to me."

"Mirabelle cares only for power and money. If she could get them by returning you to your father…" I stopped when I saw the way she wrung her hands in her lap. "I'm sure he promised her a handsome reward."

For one heart-stopping moment, I thought she would cry. Instead, she whispered a soft "Thank you."

I exhaled and took several deep breaths.

"I should have known. Why would someone like Mirabelle want to befriend me?"

I cursed under my breath and moved to sit next to her. "It has nothing to do with you. Mirabelle is used to being cast aside when men tire of her." I hesitated, choosing my words carefully. "For that reason, she has always had to put herself first. I'm sure she told herself she was doing you a favor. In her warped mind, she would have justified her actions. She wouldn't see it as a betrayal. No doubt she thought she was returning you to your proper position in society."

A shudder went through Victoria's body. Her chest rose as she took a deep breath and released it. "I won't make the same mistake again."

A strange sensation twisted inside me. I felt like a monster who'd just kicked a small kitten. The fire had gone out of her, and she deflated so completely. It nearly undid me when she looked away.

"This isn't your fault, Victoria. You see the best in people, and I admire that. But it is also true that you aren't used to the machinations of powerful men. You've only seen how Sherbourne behaves as a father." I took her hand. "You haven't seen how he behaves toward others, the ruthlessness with which he pursues his interests."

She was unnaturally still. I waited until she turned to look at me. I still held her hand, and our knees touched.

Her voice was barely above a whisper when she spoke. "If Father had succeeded today, I would be taken back to our house in Mayfair. Then..." She took another deep breath. "Dr. Mullins would be waiting to check the state of my maidenhead."

A savage curse tore from my lips as I pictured the

scene. The way the man would spread her legs apart, examine her, then pronounce judgment. Her father would be delighted. Then he would lock her away. There would be no servants like Lily to bring her even a modicum of human comfort, no second chances.

I tightened my grip on her hand and forced myself to relax. "We stopped that from happening. And now that you know the lengths to which he will go, it won't happen again."

She stared wordlessly at me, her expression unreadable. Then something flickered within the depths of her eyes.

"Tell me what you're thinking."

Her lips pressed together, as though she meant to refuse. Then, finally, she placed her other hand over mine, where I held hers.

"You need to take my maidenhead."

Despite the fact that Victoria's voice was low, barely audible, her words seemed to echo through the carriage. Or perhaps they merely echoed inside my head. From the moment our eyes met across the billiard room at King's, we were always headed here. I had tried to convince myself that I wouldn't touch her because she was Rexford's sister, but that had always been a lie.

I wasn't noble. I took what I wanted. And I wanted Victoria.

Still, I couldn't forget my promise to Rexford that I wouldn't hurt her. I'd initiated her into the world of passion last night, showing a restraint I'd never managed with any other woman. But I needed to be sure she wouldn't regret it.

I brought our joined hands to my lips and dropped a kiss there. "There's no going back from that."

Her gaze softened. "I know."

I searched her eyes for even a hint of trepidation. "If at any point you want me to stop, just say the word."

She smiled. "I trust you, and I do want this. Last night showed me that I want to be with you more than I could have imagined."

I swallowed hard and tried to curb the lust that raged inside me. It was almost impossible to keep from plucking her off the bench and spreading her thighs over my lap. But we weren't out of danger yet. I had to keep my wits about me in case we were being followed. I knew Rexford sent additional men, but his father was equally determined to retrieve his daughter. It was not the time for distractions. We sat next to each other, me holding one of her hands on my lap while I forced myself to look out the window for any indication that we were being pursued.

We made it to the townhouse safely, and I escorted Victoria inside. My tension didn't ease until the door was locked behind us.

"Go upstairs. I'll meet you there in a few minutes."

She nodded and turned away.

I watched her climb the stairs to her bedroom before finally turning to the butler. "We might have trouble tonight. Sherbourne attempted to regain control of his daughter, and he now knows where she's staying."

The man nodded, his expression grave. "I understand. I will ensure everyone is awake and alert for any signs of difficulty."

I nodded. "Thank you. Do you know if Rexford has any pistols in the townhouse?"

"A set of dueling pistols are locked in the bottom drawer of the library desk, my lord."

He reached for a set of keys in his coat pocket and separated one from the bunch. I nodded my thanks and headed to the library. The cool, logical side of my brain told me that no one would make it through the front door of the townhouse.

Still, the sun would set soon enough, and they might attempt by stealth what they weren't brave enough to do during daylight hours. Sherbourne wouldn't want to cause further scandal, but that didn't mean he would give up.

And if someone did manage to enter the house, I would be prepared.

CHAPTER 27

VICTORIA

Moreland was going to take my maidenhead. It was still late afternoon, but I'd learned from Mirabelle that men and women didn't need to wait until nightfall to share a bed. I was very glad for that knowledge because I didn't want to wait a minute longer.

Lily helped me into a demure nightgown. She tried to convince me to wear one of the more risqué garments Madame Argent had sent, but I wasn't ready for that. Perhaps, in time, I would have the confidence to wear them, but not tonight.

When she left, I turned toward the bed and

waited for a hint of uncertainty or fear. Instead of doubt, all I felt was anticipation. Last night, after Moreland left, I'd dreamed that he had stayed with me and pleasured me all night.

I wanted to touch him, something he'd denied me. Smiling, I slipped under the covers. Moreland would be here soon enough, and this time, he wouldn't stop.

The only other man who'd ever touched me intimately was the physician father had employed to check on the state of my maidenhead. I had despised the man's cold, perfunctory touch. Lily had overseen the interaction, and I'd felt nothing but shame throughout the entire ordeal. But last night, when Moreland had touched me, the feelings he'd wrung from my body had been unexpected. I was eager to experience it again.

Several minutes passed, and I began to wonder if he'd changed his mind. Or worse. Perhaps Father's men had followed the carriage and were demanding entry. A moment of panic speared through me, but I pushed it away. Lily would have returned if that was happening. She'd saved me once before, and I knew she was committed to keeping me safe. And hot on her heels would be Moreland. He wouldn't allow my father to take me.

I covered my face with my hands as embarrassment filled me. I'd behaved foolishly today. Mirabelle had even hinted about her motives in the carriage. Now that our outing had been revealed in a new light, I recognized the strange emotion I'd seen cross her face—guilt. She wasn't the hardhearted woman Moreland thought her, but she was solely responsible for her own safety. I could only pity her. After this whole thing was over, I would still be able to count on my brother to keep me safe. Mirabelle could only ever rely on herself.

A soft knock sounded at the door, and I took a steadying breath before bidding the person to enter. When the door swung open, Moreland stood at the threshold, staring at me.

His gaze took in my position on the bed. After staring at me, he walked into the room and placed a case on my dressing table. I hadn't seen it before and didn't know what was inside. Whatever it was, he left it there, then turned to lock my bedchamber door.

He turned to look at me again, one corner of his mouth tilting upward. That smile at once eased my nerves and heightened my anticipation. I sat up and waited, unsure about how to proceed. I was proving to be a poor mistress, but after tonight, I hoped I would have the confidence to properly continue my relationship with Moreland. We would be bound together for a few weeks at least—or I hoped that would be true. I planned to make use of the time we had together to forge memories that would last me a lifetime.

"Last chance to change your mind, Victoria."

I met his gaze, and my voice was unwavering. "I want this more than you could imagine. And not because of what happened today. I won't change my mind."

He walked farther into the room, his steps silent. I watched the graceful way he moved as he stripped off his tailcoat and raised a hand to his cravat. I was mesmerized as he undid the fabric's knot and pulled it loose. He dropped it onto the chair at my dressing table and draped his coat over the back.

I was enthralled as he continued. He undid the buttons of his waistcoat and removed it with care before adding it to the growing pile of clothes on the chair. I waited to see if he would remove his shirt next. Without his waistcoat and the cravat, it gaped loose at the neck. I could see the hint of muscles and chest hair peeking from beneath the fabric. I hadn't known that men had hair on their chest, but I couldn't wait to see just how different his body was from mine.

Instead of removing his shirt, he moved his hands to his breeches. When he pulled the garment down and removed his shoes and stockings, the edge of his shirt covered him to the tops of his thighs. He stood like that, staring at me.

I licked my suddenly dry lips. "Are you—are you going to remove your shirt?" I phrased it as a question, but I meant it as a demand.

His brow quirked upward, and he folded his arms across his chest. "I'll remove my shirt when you remove your nightdress."

Summoning my courage, I turned down the coverlet and stood. We were facing each other now, only a few feet separating us.

"That's not fair, my lord. You are the more experienced person here. I am but a shy maiden."

He laughed and held out a hand. "Come here."

I obeyed his command without question and allowed him to draw me into his embrace. It was where I wanted to be, after all—in his arms. I lifted my face and rose onto my tiptoes just as he leaned down and took my mouth in a heated kiss.

Any uncertainty I'd harbored vanished. The sun

hadn't set yet, and it was scandalous to do this before nightfall, but I didn't care.

He deepened the kiss, and I wrapped my arms around his neck. With a gruff sound, he placed his arms under my backside, and it was only then that I realized he'd been inching up the fabric of my nightdress. I'd been so distracted by the way he kissed me, the feel of his muscular chest against mine and the hard length of him pressing against me. He lifted me with surprising ease, and some instinct had me wrapping my legs around his waist. When he pulled back to look down at me, his eyes were dark.

"I'm not going to stop, Victoria."

I grinned. "Good. I don't want you to."

And with that, we tumbled onto the bed.

With a flurry of movement, he carefully lifted my nightdress. I was too distracted by my own task of divesting him of his shirt. My hands trembled but not because I was afraid. I didn't think I'd ever wanted anything more than what was happening between us.

His gaze swept over my body. "I've been thinking about what it would be like to see you like this. Leaving you last night was the hardest thing I've ever had to do."

He might have been content to look for the moment, but I was eager to touch him. I started at his shoulders, enjoying the way his hard flesh felt under my fingertips. I moved down to his chest, exploring the muscles beneath the hair that covered him there. My touch trailed down to his abdomen, where the hair tapered to a fine line leading farther down.

His hands covered mine, and our eyes met. He didn't have to ask the question.

"I want to do this."

He nodded and released me. I looked down for the first time at the hard length of him. I wasn't completely innocent. After my conversation with Mirabelle yesterday, I'd summoned the courage to ask Lily a few questions this morning. She had filled in the blanks in my knowledge about what happened between a man and a woman.

Lily hadn't been surprised by my questions, and I realized the staff already knew that Moreland and I were no longer pretending that I was his mistress. But my maid's roundabout descriptions of what would happen tonight hadn't prepared me for this.

I looked up at him. "Is that supposed to fit inside me?"

He laughed and rolled us over. I was on my back now, and he hovered over me.

"It will fit," he said and kissed me again.

I'd meant to touch him, give him some of the same pleasure he'd shown me last night, but the feel of his heated body touching me everywhere erased all thoughts. I became pure sensation, relishing the way his hands traced over my body as I explored the muscles along his back. When his hand moved between us, I opened my legs. I already knew what would happen.

"I'm ready," I said when his fingers found me.

He stared down at me. "I'll make sure of it." Then he started kissing his way down my body.

He spent some time kissing and caressing my breasts. When he spread my legs farther and stared up at me from between them, I remembered something that Mirabelle had shared with me. But she'd also told me that most men didn't like doing that.

I was about to tell him that he didn't have to do anything he didn't want to, but then his mouth was on me, and I was incapable of speech. The sounds I made should have embarrassed me, but I was beyond shame. When he eased one, then two fingers inside me and curled them against me, pleasure crashed through me, and I called out his name.

I hadn't thought myself capable of surpassing the ecstasy he'd shown me last night, but I was clearly mistaken. If he continued along his current trajectory, then lovemaking would be even better.

He lifted himself over me, his face serious. "This might hurt."

"Because it's too big?"

A surprised chuckle escaped him. "No, Victoria, not because I'm too big. Because this is your first time. But I promise that next time, it will be easier."

I nodded my understanding, but my mind was fixed on the inherent promise of those words. Next time. He wouldn't bed me then grow bored and move on to another woman. Not right away. It was his way of promising that he would stay with me for a little while.

He kissed me as he fit his hard length along my folds. I'd enjoyed the way his fingers and mouth felt when he'd touched me there, but this was something altogether new. It was as though my body knew what was about to happen and was desperate for him to make love to me.

I felt a sharp pinch of pain as he thrust into me, then he stilled.

I panted. "That did hurt."

"I know." He rested his forehead against mine and waited. "Tell me when I can move."

I was a little afraid to move myself, but true to his word, he remained still, though I could see the strain in the clench of his jaw and the way he closed his eyes. I didn't know how long we stayed like that before I realized the pain had passed, but I felt full. I clenched around him, and he groaned.

"Victoria…"

"You can move," I said.

"Thank God." He pulled out slowly, then eased back inside me, much more slowly than he had the first time.

I tensed, waiting for the pain to return, but none came. When he did it a second time and pressed his thumb on that spot where he'd placed his mouth before, pleasure raced through me. I couldn't hold back my whimper.

He started moving faster then. The more he pushed into me, the greater my excitement rose. When he'd used his mouth, my relief had been swift. But this time, it was a slow build. My body reached a height that I feared would kill me.

"Moreland," I said, "I don't know if I can—"

"You can." He angled his hips and hit a space inside me that caused a shock of sensation to pierce me. His thumb kept moving against me, and over-whelming euphoria crashed through me. My entire body tensed, and I saw stars behind my closed lids.

He groaned as he pushed himself all the way inside me. Then he swore as he pulled out. I could feel his release against my belly. Lily had told me about it—that she would find something I could use to help prevent me from falling with child, but that I needed to be careful because if he spent himself inside me, it might happen. I had completely forgotten her warning. Thank goodness Moreland had his wits about him.

He kissed me softly. "Stay here." He stood, and I watched him stride to the washbasin set up behind a dressing screen. The play of muscles on his back-side was surprisingly pleasant to witness. He returned with a washcloth and cleaned up the mess he'd made on my stomach.

"Do you want me to…?" He indicated between my legs.

"No." I shook my head. "I'll do it."

He smiled a little. "There's blood there. Not a lot, but…"

I nodded. "I know."

I waited for him to turn around, but when he didn't, I gathered my courage and moved to the dressing area. I was glad for the privacy of the screen as I cleaned myself. When I returned, I gasped when I saw the blood on the coverlet.

He was correct when he'd said there wasn't much, but it was still shocking.

"Come here," he said, pulling down the fabric.

I slid into bed. Moreland stayed standing, looking down at me. I held my breath as I waited to see if he would join me. When he walked away, my heart sank.

But instead of making his way to where he'd left his clothing, he moved to the dressing area, and I realized he must be cleaning the blood from himself.

When he returned, he climbed into bed next to me. I moved into his arms without a word and settled against him. Contentment washed over me as he pulled my head onto his chest. I realized that this was what it felt like to be happy. I closed my eyes, memorizing the way he felt. I would relish this moment for the rest of my life.

CHAPTER 28

MORELAND

It seemed I was incapable of letting this woman out of my sight. I'd breached my tenuous grasp on my restraint, and I was no longer capable of holding back.

I expected Victoria to protest when I kept her in bed for the rest of the evening, but she surprised me. She was the one who called for her maid to have dinner brought up to us.

I didn't make love to her again. She would be too sore after I'd taken her maidenhead. But I'd already initiated her into some of the other ways of giving pleasure, and she was an apt student.

The damnable thing was that I enjoyed being in her company far too much. For one so young, she was surprisingly well-read. And she had a knowledge of horrid novels that surprised me.

My education had centered on the classics, but she insisted on telling me most animatedly about all I was missing. I had the errant thought that I could easily grow addicted to having her recount the details of all the ridiculous plots in so many of those stories.

She scrunched her nose when I remarked on one particularly ridiculous novel about a young woman trapped in a cliffside castle with a brooding older hero. "The situation isn't that different from the one in which I now find myself."

I smirked, conceding the point. "At least here, there are no mysterious moans in the middle of the night or rattling of chains."

"Well," she said, "there have been no moans up to this point."

With that, she began an exploration of my body while I lay there and waited to see what she would do. I was, of course, hard when she finally touched me. Her mouth formed a little O of interest, and I had to close my eyes at the sight.

I definitely wanted to do other things with

Victoria but not yet. Despite everything we'd shared, she was still far too innocent. I didn't want her to be just another woman with whom I sated my desires. I was fond of her, and that was a dangerous discovery.

We didn't leave her room until the following morning, when we headed downstairs for breakfast. I waited for her to fill her plate, then did the same. My emotions had been in turmoil yesterday after nearly losing Victoria. But when I woke this morning, it was with certainty that we had only one way to assure she would stay safe.

She took a sip of her tea, narrowing her eyes at me over the cup's rim. "You seem to be pondering something." She set the cup on its saucer. "If it's about my careless behavior yesterday, you can rest assured that I won't leave the house again without you or my brother."

I shook my head. Victoria wouldn't make the same mistake twice. "I'm not worried about that. But I must admit that Mirabelle surprised me as well. I didn't think her capable of such betrayal."

Victoria bit her bottom lip, then sighed. "I believe she convinced herself that she was helping me."

I'd suggested as much to her yesterday when

she'd learned of Mirabelle's betrayal, but I couldn't believe it was true. "Or she was helping herself to the reward that Sherbourne no doubt offered her."

Victoria winced. "Perhaps. But during her initial visit, she told me about her first protector, and the memory made her sad. I don't think she wanted this life. She was once a young woman who dreamed of finding true love." She shook her head. "You've seen how beautiful she is, and her family didn't have money. So, while men were interested in her, their intentions weren't honorable."

I could imagine all too well the situation that had led to Mirabelle's downfall. But she'd landed on her feet and was no victim. Still, I couldn't help but remember the article in *The Mayfair Chronicle* about a potential marriage between her and Kendrick. Was she still hoping to find a man who would save her from her current life?

"Her intentions don't matter. We both know that you're much better off with me than in your father's care. He clearly isn't looking for someone who will see to your emotional well-being when you marry."

She shuddered. "Lord Heddington would have just one use for me. Well, perhaps two. Giving him children and acting as a hostess for his guests."

I didn't want to think about how close she'd come to marrying that man. If Rexford hadn't installed people in his father's house to look after his sister, nothing could have stopped Sherbourne.

"So, what were you considering so earnestly, my lord?" She watched me as she nibbled a corner of her toast.

I stared down at my full plate, realizing that my hunger had vanished. I knew this day would arrive, but I'd thought I had years ahead of me.

"I think you and I should marry."

Victoria paused, her eyes opening wide with shock, then she burst into laughter. I waited, feeling far from amused. But I had to concede that it was understandable that she would think my offer wasn't real.

When she realized I wasn't laughing or even smiling, she sobered. "You're having fun at my expense, are you not?"

I raised a brow. "I must admit, I never expected that, when I proposed, it would be met with such amusement."

"But you're one of the Legendary Lords. You don't offer women proposals of marriage."

My gaze remained fixed on her. "Clearly, that isn't true."

She frowned, and I wondered what was happening in that distractingly attractive head of hers. I should have realized that she was too smart not to consider the possibility that I was only offering her marriage out of a sense of duty.

"No." She shook her head and pushed her plate away. She took another sip of tea, then carefully placed the cup back on the saucer before meeting my gaze again. "I don't expect such a sacrifice from you. I know that me acting as your mistress—" She waved her hands, becoming animated on the subject matter. "You've admitted that you've never had a mistress before, but you do have a reputation as a rake." Her mouth firmed into a line.

"And what, Victoria? Go ahead and ask me what it is you want to know."

She let out a shaky breath. "I don't think I could be married to you and find myself alone at home while you…" She waved her hands again.

"While I what, exactly?"

She made a soft sound of disgust. "While you continued bedding other women."

It was a valid concern, and I could certainly see why she would believe such a thing of me. "My father was a philanderer."

Both her brows shot up at my admission. I'd

never offered her information about my family before. I didn't like speaking about them.

"And that is why you're one as well?"

"No." I frowned. "My father…" I shrugged. "I wouldn't be surprised if I have quite a few half brothers and sisters. I've never met them, but from what my mother has implied, it wouldn't be outside the realm of possibility. Still, I saw how unhappy my father's infidelities made my mother. When my parents passed away…"

I stopped, my mind shying from wanting to share the circumstances surrounding their deaths. The carriage ride had been deemed an accident, but a part of me had always wondered if that was true. My father had been driving my mother in a phaeton, which she hated. And given how the two argued, I wouldn't be surprised if my father had caused the accident, intending to hurt my mother. He'd always been less than kind to her.

"I have been… free with my attention when it came to the fairer sex because I always knew that when I married, I wouldn't cause my wife similar pain."

It wasn't an admission of love. I wasn't sure I was capable of that. But Victoria had shown me that I *was* capable of fondness and fidelity. It would be no sacrifice being married to her.

Her eyes widened with shock. "And you would be fine with that?"

I leaned back in my chair, folded my arms across my chest, and didn't try to hide my amusement. "I think you and I have proven to one another that we are quite compatible in the bedroom. And that was just the beginning."

Her cheeks reddened. "I don't know. Would Rexford allow it?" Then she gasped. "I am still underage. My father will never grant his permission."

"I know. We'll need to speak with your brother. Perhaps we can do something to change his mind."

"We could elope," Victoria said.

I'd already considered that possibility. "It might still come to that. But we'll go to King's after breakfast and speak to your brother. He's proven resourceful when it comes to outsmarting your father."

CHAPTER 29

VICTORIA

Moreland wanted to marry me. We hadn't known each other long, but I felt a bone deep certainty that I wanted to be his wife.

I scrunched my nose as a thought occurred to me. We were alone in the carriage, but I'd seen the veritable army of outriders that had followed us from the house. We'd set out as soon as breakfast was finished. It was still early, and the streets were quiet, but if Father knew where I was, his own men would be watching the house. And they would have seen our departure. I didn't want to think about the possibility that my father's men could be following us, waiting for an opportunity to snatch me away from Moreland.

"If we are to be married, I should know your Christian name."

For a moment, I thought he wouldn't reply, but then, with a small shrug, he said, "Matthew."

"Matthew," I repeated. I liked it. It humanized him, making him seem less a Legend and more a regular man.

The carriage ride from the townhouse to my brother's club was short, just ten minutes from Grosvenor Square to Saint James Street. Father had been incensed when Rexford chose to open his own club within walking distance of White's instead of falling in line and joining Father's more established club.

From what I'd come to know about my brother in the short time we'd been reacquainted, I imagined he chosen the location for King's deliberately. Every time Father visited White's, he couldn't help but see his son's club. Surely, Rexford enjoyed being a constant source of annoyance for our father. I couldn't blame him. I felt a thrill at the knowledge that I was free from Father's control.

But unlike Rexford, my situation was far more

tenuous. I couldn't do much for myself and had to rely on him and Moreland.

I stared at Moreland from across the carriage. I wasn't foolish enough to expect him to fall in love with me, but I could be content in the union if he kept his promise to remain faithful.

He returned my gaze, and I watched his expression grow heated. No doubt he was remembering the intimacies we'd shared. And in that moment, I realized that I loved him. I wanted him to be happy, and I vowed to do everything in my power to make that a reality.

The carriage slowed and drove around to the back of the club, where my brother kept his stables. It was a luxury in that part of London, but one I was very thankful for because it meant I wouldn't have to risk being seen entering King's on Moreland's arm.

When you're married, it won't matter who sees you. I smiled at the thought, wanting that beyond anything. But I knew Father would never give his consent, which meant we would have to elope.

When the carriage door opened, Moreland jumped down and turned around to help me out. His hands remained on my waist when I reached the ground.

"What are you thinking?" he asked.

I smiled and leaned in close. "I'm thinking about how much I'm looking forward to being alone with you again."

He dropped a quick kiss on my lips and turned to lead me into the club. Mr. Clarence was just arriving to greet us.

He bowed in my direction. "It's a pleasure to see you again, Lady Victoria."

I beamed at the older man. My memories of his time as Father's steward were vague, but I did recall that he'd always been kind. I didn't know why he'd left my father's employment, but I was glad that he worked for Rexford.

We followed him through the club's back entrance.

"Is anyone else here?" Moreland asked.

Mr. Clarence shook his head. "This early in the morning, it's only Lord Rexford."

Moreland nodded. "That's probably for the best."

Mr. Clarence led the way up the back stairs to my brother's study and rapped twice on the door. Rexford called out, and Mr. Clarence opened the door for us.

When he saw us, Rexford stood and gathered me against him.

"I was so relieved that Moreland could get to you before Father."

I wrapped my arms around his waist, returning his embrace. "I'm sorry for all the trouble I gave you yesterday. I wasn't thinking clearly."

Rexford pulled back, his expression somber. "None of us were. I should have realized that Father would recruit allies from among our acquaintances."

"Well, I definitely learned my lesson."

When he smiled down at me, I was thankful that he didn't resemble our father. We both resembled our mother, who was dark haired and shared our blue eyes. Father's eyes were a lighter shade of blue, icy-cold eyes that bored straight through a person. His hair was gray, but I remembered it being a much lighter shade of brown when I was a girl.

Moreland took my hand in his. "I need to speak to your brother concerning what we discussed this morning. Do you wish to stay?"

My heart lifted at the way he looked down at me as he waited for my reply. I was accustomed to having others determine my future for me. Before escaping my father's household, no one had ever asked me what I wanted.

"The two of you will need to strategize because this won't be easy. I don't need to know the details. I trust you."

Moreland squeezed my hand before releasing it.

I followed Mr. Clarence to the small sitting room I'd occupied the last time I came, when Rexford had first explained his plan to ruin my reputation. Now, I waited again as he and Moreland discussed how they could salvage my reputation by making me a baroness. The irony wasn't lost on me.

I sighed and turned to Mr. Clarence. "Thank you again for everything you've done. I'm afraid I've been quite a burden to all of you."

Mr. Clarence stood before me, his hands clutched behind his back. I couldn't decipher his gaze as he continued to stare at me. I'd noticed it before. If I had to describe it, I would say he was trying to memorize my features.

"You never have to apologize," he said.

"But something is the matter." My voice was soft. "You appear distraught."

He smiled then. "You look just like your mother.

She was beautiful and kind, and I admired her greatly."

My heart stuttered at the obvious fondness in his voice. Father never spoke about my mother, who had died when I was still a child. "I don't remember much about her. Only that she had dark hair and that she was often sad."

His brows drew together. "Yes, she was. I'm afraid her marriage to your father wasn't a happy one."

I wasn't surprised to hear that.

He took a step closer. "I vow that I will do everything in my power to keep you safe. She would have wanted that."

His earnest tone had me wondering what exactly he could have witnessed between my parents that had him so desperate to protect me. I almost asked him, but fear stopped me.

I didn't want to know how horribly Father treated my mother. "Thank you, Mr. Clarence."

He nodded. "I will have the staff bring you some refreshments." With a fond smile, he turned and left the room.

I watched him go, wondering about all the secrets Mr. Clarence must be privy to, both past and present. I couldn't help but hope that Mr. Clarence had been a friend to my mother all those years ago when she'd so desperately needed one.

CHAPTER 30

MORELAND

I watched Victoria leave Rexford's study with Clarence, fighting back the urge to go after her. She was safe here. Logically, I knew that. But the previous day's close call had shaken me badly. I didn't want to let her out of my sight.

"You care for her."

I'd almost forgotten Rexford was there. Instead of racing after Victoria, I forced myself to turn and face her brother. Rexford had always been astute—one of the traits that made him so formidable.

"You charged me with seeing to her safety. And

yesterday…" I shook my head. "I was almost too late. I intercepted her right outside the dressmaker's shop."

Rexford leaned back against his desk, his hands gripping the surface behind him. "I was about to go myself. When you stormed out of here—"

I met his gaze. "Why didn't you?"

He watched me intently. "I was testing a theory."

Rexford's words didn't sit well with me. Against my will, my hands clenched at my sides. "Testing a theory? What theory was that? Who would come out ahead? Tell me you haven't placed a bet on what's going to happen to Victoria."

He folded his arms across his chest and continued to examine me. He seemed far too calm for my liking.

"Watching you race from here, I knew you had the situation well in hand. Don't forget, I've seen you in the boxing ring. And I did send men after you."

I forced myself to relax my fists and shook out my hands. Rexford was correct, after all. We didn't both need to be there, and he'd sent a small army after me.

"I'm going to repeat my question," Rexford said. "Do you care for her?"

I could no longer lie to myself. I did have feelings for her. Somewhere along the way, I'd developed a fondness for Victoria that baffled me, which made my plan tolerable. I'd always assumed that when I wedded, it would be to a woman I could tolerate. But with Victoria… we could be happy together. I enjoyed her company, and I *wanted* to make her happy. It was the most damnable thing.

"Moreland," Rexford prodded.

I met his gaze. "Yes, I care for her."

Rexford's smile was small but satisfied. "Why are you two here today? Have you come to ask me to whisk Victoria away to the country?"

I almost recoiled at the thought. It was within Rexford's power to do that, and I wasn't sure I could stop him.

"Quite the opposite," I said. "Victoria and I discussed the matter this morning."

"And?"

"We've decided to wed."

I don't know what I expected. A frown, perhaps. At the very least, surprise. Instead, Rexford's face remained a smooth, unreadable mask.

"I see. And what does my sister have to say about this?"

"She's worried that your father won't agree to the match, and since she's not yet of age…"

"That is a stumbling block. So, it seems we shall have to hide Victoria in the country after all." Rexford straightened and started to make his way around his desk.

But before he could sit, I grasped his arm and turned him around. "No. We will elope if we have to."

Rexford examined my face. When his gaze dropped to my hand, I released him.

"What if I told you that one of the other Legends has offered to marry Victoria in your stead?"

I felt Rexford's words like a blow. "You don't think I'm good enough for her."

His expression didn't change. "That's not what I said."

"Then what exactly do you mean by that? You've already spoken to someone else about marrying her? I was good enough to make her my mistress but not good enough to marry her?"

Rexford met my gaze. "I can always count on you."

I shook my head. "What does that mean?"

"It means," Rexford continued, "that you have never said no to one of my requests. You are always there, no matter what the demand, but I don't want you to sacrifice the rest of your life just to please me."

"And yet you're fine asking one of the others?"

"No," Rexford said. "I haven't spoken about marriage to anyone. I just wanted to see your reaction."

I took a step back. "I don't understand what's happening here."

"I don't want to force you to marry my sister, but I know that if I asked it of you, you would do it. That is a sacrifice I would never impose on you. Doing so would make me exactly like Sherbourne, and we are nothing alike. I do not enjoy moving men around like pieces on a chessboard to enact my whims."

Of course not. I could clearly see Rexford's anger and frustration. His father had spent his whole life controlling him, and while I didn't know exactly what had happened, I knew that Mr. Clarence had been instrumental in helping Rexford escape.

Before Rexford had set up King's, Sherbourne

had made him dance a merry tune, playing him like a puppet master. I remembered how angry Rexford had been back then. He might be ruthless, but Rexford did not use people in that way.

We faced each other, and I straightened my shoulders. "I *want* to marry Victoria. We are compatible in all ways, and it would be my privilege to make her happy."

Rexford's eyes narrowed at that, but he said nothing.

I continued. "Even if she wasn't your sister, even if she wasn't in danger, Victoria is the woman I want as my wife."

He examined me for several seconds, then nodded. "I see. You'll understand why I need to speak to her before giving my consent."

I nodded. "I would expect nothing less."

"Stay here. I will speak to her, and if she agrees, we'll need to figure out how to bring this about. Hopefully, it can be managed without you two fleeing to Scotland tonight."

I watched him leave the room. When five minutes had passed, I began to pace. My worry grew. Perhaps I hadn't convinced him that I was acting entirely of my own volition. What if he was in there trying to convince Victoria that we shouldn't wed?

I sank into one of the armchairs that Rexford had provided for when the Legends met and forced myself to wait, though every instinct screamed at me to barge into that sitting room. I trusted Victoria. She wouldn't allow Rexford to send her away.

The door opened, and I rose. Rexford stepped into the room, followed by Victoria. The three of us stayed like that for one heart-stopping moment before Victoria smiled and stepped into my arms.

"We're going to get married."

I smiled down at her, relief and an emotion that felt perilously close to happiness filling me. "Yes, we are."

I didn't know how long we remained that way before Rexford cleared his throat. For the second time, I'd forgotten he was in the room. What was it about this woman that had me so singularly focused on her?

Rexford was clearly amused. "How are we going to gain Sherbourne's agreement?"

"I have an idea."

We both stared at Victoria, who shrugged.

"I had time to think while I was waiting for you

two." She looked at Rexford. "Father is wary of crossing one man. If we can elicit his assistance…"

Rexford grinned. "Of course."

I looked between them. "And who would that be?"

"Lord Brantford," they said in unison.

VICTORIA

The atmosphere within the carriage on the way home was tense, the silence heavy. Moreland sat next to me, and seated across from us were two large men who I'd been informed were necessary for our safety. The outriders who had accompanied the carriage earlier still followed us, but the two who rode with us were a last line of defense if my father tried to overtake the carriage.

I had to call upon all my training to mask the turmoil swirling within me. I thought I'd been successful. When we entered the house, the butler assured us that everything had been quiet. Moreland took my hand and led me upstairs. He closed my bedroom door and turned to face me.

"Try not to worry," he said.

I let out a shaky laugh. "Am I that bad at hiding my emotions?"

His smile was soft. "You wouldn't be the person I've come to know if you weren't a little upset."

"And who is that?"

He took my hands and drew me closer. "You care. You're worried about the difficulties our marriage might cause me and wondering if you should give me my freedom."

I'd been trying so hard not to think about the corner I'd forced Moreland into, but I could no longer pretend it didn't exist. "I know you told me that you didn't mind, but Father will try to ruin you. I'm sure he's already setting things in motion with that end in mind."

He tugged me against his chest, and I came willingly. I wrapped my arms around his neck, enjoying the weight of his hands on my waist.

"It's not merely a matter of me not minding. I *want* to marry you."

A thrill settled through me at his words, but I found it impossible to forget that he was accustomed to being with many women. "I'll try not to bore you or be too demanding of your time. You're used to—"

He dropped a quick kiss on my lips. "I want you to be yourself."

I shook my head. "I'm not sure who that is. I've been raised to be Lord Sherbourne's dutiful daughter, the perfect hostess, and a credit to his name and to my future husband."

He frowned. "You can rest assured that I won't be hosting any balls or social gatherings."

I laughed, aiming for levity. "Well, there goes all my usefulness."

He grinned, a mischievous twinkle entering his eyes. "I think we can find a few things you could do to hold my interest."

Awareness flooded through me, but I couldn't help teasing him. "I don't know, my lord. What if I tire of your attention?"

His head lowered, and his mouth hovered over my ear, the soft breath causing shivers to race through me. "I can't have that. We'll have to see what I can do to remedy your concerns."

I didn't know what possessed me to reach up onto my tiptoes and whisper into his ear. "I'm no longer sore from last night."

He reared back and stared down at me, then his

mouth curled up in that wicked grin of his I'd come to love so much.

Our mouths came together in an explosive kiss. It had only been hours, but my body yearned for him. Moreland was going to be my husband. We would have years together.

Despite what he'd said, I found it difficult to believe that he wouldn't tire of me. I wasn't entirely innocent and knew that few husbands remained faithful to their wives. But I no longer cared. I would take whatever he chose to share with me now and treasure the memories later.

He walked me backward across the room. I didn't see where he was leading me, but I assumed it was the bed. I was surprised, therefore, to feel the dressing table against my backside. He trailed a line of kisses up to my ear.

"Turn around, Victoria. I want you to see what I'm about to do to you."

I obeyed without thinking, and our eyes met and held in the dressing table mirror.

It was all new to me. I wasn't sure what he planned to do, but I watched as he unpinned my hair, tossing the hairpins onto the surface of the vanity.

His eyes remained fixed on my dark hair as it

fell down my back. Then he swept it to one side and gathered it in his palm while his other hand reached around to span my waist. He pressed me back against him, and I could feel the hard length of his arousal against my lower back.

When he kissed the side of my neck, I made a soft sound of pleasure and tilted my head to give him better access. His hands were all over me then, cupping my breasts as his hips pressed me into the dressing table. I watched his hands in the mirror, and when I looked up to see what he was thinking, I realized that his gaze had been fixed on my face the entire time, taking in every expression.

I felt more exposed than I had last night when I'd stripped bare for him. We were both fully clothed, but something about what we were doing now seemed more intimate.

My thoughts scattered, and I became pure sensation as I watched his hands gather the fabric of my skirts and slowly start to drag up the material. I should have been embarrassed when my bare legs came into view. I watched him reach between my thighs to touch me there, where he'd already shown me that the center of my pleasure lay. But instead of embarrassment, the sight only increased my desire.

What we were doing was wicked, but I didn't care. I would never be able to say no to him because I wanted what was happening between us just as much as he did.

He lowered his mouth to my ear. "Lean forward, love."

The endearment caused a pang to settle in my heart. He didn't mean it, of course. Moreland didn't love me. But I did love him, and in that moment, I could pretend that he felt the same way.

I obeyed and watched as he undid the fall of his trousers. I couldn't see exactly what he was doing, but his motions were undeniable.

Last night, we'd been naked when we made love, but we were still fully dressed when I felt the hard length of him against my slick arousal. I moaned his name, my voice low and raspy.

"Shh." He dropped another kiss on the side of my throat, then he pushed into me.

I gasped at the sudden intrusion. But not in pain. No, he felt good, and I wanted this more than I'd ever thought possible. He'd shown me desire and fulfillment with his hands and his mouth. Then last night he'd made love to me, but there had been some pain in the beginning. Today, there was only pleasure.

He held my hips and rocked into me again. "Open your eyes."

I was so intent on the way he felt, I hadn't realized that I'd closed them. I bit my lip and met his gaze in the mirror.

"What are you feeling?" he asked. "Is this"—he surged into me harder—"too much?"

Again, I let out a soft cry. "No," I said between pants. "Keep going. Don't stop."

He picked up speed, and I met his rocking movement with the backward thrust of my hips.

He let out a low groan and reached around to touch me just above where our bodies were joined. A soft flick of his fingers was all it took for me to shatter into a million pieces. His eyes never left mine, then he gripped my hips again, holding me still as he reached his own release. We stayed like that, our breathing beginning to slow, as he softened and slipped out of me.

Then he closed his eyes and swore. "I'm sorry. I should have pulled out."

I turned around and hugged him, my thoughts going back to the conversation I'd had with Lily. "Nothing might come of it."

He remained still, staring down at me.

I tried to ignore my alarm. "We will be married

soon, so it would be fine if I fell pregnant with your child."

He stiffened, and for a moment, I was afraid that I'd said the wrong thing.

Finally, he nodded and gathered me into his arms. "I think I'd like that."

CHAPTER 32

MORELAND

Rexford's note arrived three days later. He'd managed to secure an appointment with the Earl of Brantford. While we'd waited for word, I hadn't left Victoria's side.

I was slowly coming to terms with the fact that instead of growing bored, I was more determined than ever to make her my wife. Normally, I didn't find women who were newly out in society all that interesting. But Victoria's depth of character intrigued me. She tried so hard to be self-reliant, and I knew it was because she didn't want to be a burden. It was the most confounding thing, but the more she tried to pull away, the more I wanted to keep her close.

And now that I'd had her in my bed, I couldn't stand the thought of anyone else touching her. She was mine, and I intended to keep her.

I didn't know what Rexford had to promise Brantford to gain an audience, but the two men held a great deal of influence. It made sense that Brantford, who seemed to have the ear of everyone in government, if not in the royal family itself, would see the benefit of making an alliance with the Marquess of Rexford.

It was midday when we left the townhouse and set out for Brantford's home in Mayfair. It was a short carriage ride, and under any other circumstances, I would have suggested that we walk. But Brantford's townhouse was very close to the Duke of Sherbourne's London house.

When we passed the house, the same one from which Victoria had escaped, she reached for my hand. I pulled her against my side and dropped a kiss onto her hair. Given the close call she'd had mere days before, she would have needed an admirable amount of courage to accompany me today.

She held her breath, but two minutes later,

when we stopped in front of Brantford's town-house, she'd managed to recover her equilibrium. The moment the carriage drew to a halt, she straightened and pulled away from me. Before my eyes, she transformed from the frightened young woman who was terrified that her father would find her and bring her back under his thumb to the composed daughter of a duke, who had no fear.

Someone knocked softly on the carriage door.

"Are you ready?" I asked.

She took a deep breath and nodded. I exited first, then held out my hand to help her.

The footman who'd knocked on the carriage door stood to one side, but I didn't miss the way his eyes swept up and down the street. I didn't expect Sherbourne to attempt anything on Brantford's doorstep. No one was that brave—or that foolish.

The front door was already open and a middle-aged butler stood at the threshold. I escorted Victoria into the house and handed the man my card. With a nod, he turned and led us into the drawing room. Apparently, we were the last to arrive. Rexford was already waiting, along with his right hand, Mr. Clarence. Brantford was present, as was his wife. After Rexford made the introductions,

I experienced a moment of uncertainty about what was supposed to happen now.

Before I could ask, Brantford's wife came to Victoria's side and took her other arm. "I think the men have some scheming to do," she said.

I reluctantly released her. "This involves Victoria. She should have a say in what happens."

Lady Brantford smiled warmly at me. "I agree. But for now, you can argue among yourselves about the best course of action. When you've decided on what you want to do, you can present it to her and see what she thinks."

Victoria grinned at the woman. "I think that sounds acceptable."

"Good. Now come with me. I'm sure we can find something much more entertaining to do as we become better acquainted."

I watched Victoria go, pushing back my concern. Nothing would happen to her within Brantford's home, but I hated letting her out of my sight. The last time she'd left to spend time with a friend, her father had almost succeeded in finding her.

When I turned back, everyone was watching me. I ignored them and took a seat on the settee next to Clarence. Rexford and Brantford were seated in the two armchairs.

I knew Rexford would have already outlined our situation. I couldn't imagine what he'd had to promise Brantford to gain his cooperation, but I knew that he would do anything to help his sister.

I addressed Brantford directly. "I assume you know why we're here today."

It was my first time meeting the man. The air of cool detachment about him matched his reputation. It was said that everyone wanted to be his friend but few had gained access to his inner sanctum. He normally conducted his affairs away from his wife, his actions veiled within a shroud of secrecy.

Brantford steepled his fingers and assessed me with his cold blue gaze. "Rexford has brought me up to date. You decided to ruin her, and now you want to marry her. But she is only eighteen and requires her father's permission."

I nodded.

"And you are certain that you want to marry her? It is within my means to aid in hiding her. Her father could scour the entire countryside, and I assure you she wouldn't be found."

The cool detachment with which he made that

proclamation filled me with unease. Because if Sherbourne couldn't find her, I wouldn't be able to either.

Panic threatened to take hold. "Where is she now? You're not—"

Rexford leaned forward and placed a hand on my arm, stopping me from leaping to my feet. "She hasn't been escorted out the back door."

One corner of Brantford's mouth twitched. "Indeed. My wife is a romantic. When she heard about your plight, I had no choice but to agree to assist you." He aimed an assessing glance at Rexford. "I have your friend here to blame for that."

Rexford shrugged. "We all play to our strengths, and I didn't think you would mind too much."

I half expected Brantford to call off the entire meeting. To my surprise, he smiled. "Rose is my weakness." He turned that assessing gaze back to me. "And I take it that Lady Victoria is the same for you."

Everyone was looking at me again.

"If you've changed your mind—" Rexford began.

I didn't let him finish. "No. I want to marry her, and if we have to elope, we will."

Brantford's eyes narrowed on me. "Sherbourne doesn't have the money for her dowry."

I frowned. "I don't need his money."

"True," Brantford said. "But while you may not need the money, I cannot say the same for her father. It's why he arranged Victoria's betrothal before she'd even attended her first ball this season."

The proclamation filled me with anger. "So, you're saying that he sold his daughter?"

Brantford shrugged. "Is that not what every other member of the ton does? Buy and sell their daughters' positions in society with an eye on advancing their own?"

I thought about the state of my finances. I could certainly buy her if that was what Sherbourne wanted. I could easily afford it. But Victoria was worth more than that. She wasn't a commodity to be purchased. "If you're suggesting——"

Brantford shook his head. "No, Sherbourne wants money *and* a lofty title. And I'm afraid as a baron…"

I finished his thought for him. "I'm the last person he would want for his daughter."

"Just so," Brantford said.

Rexford leaned forward. "Sherbourne has done

everything in his power to ensure no one learns about his financial constraints."

I turned to look at Clarence. He'd been Sherbourne's steward before he left to help Rexford establish King's. As far as I was aware, he'd been with Lord Sherbourne since before Rexford's birth. "Did you know about this?"

Clarence shrugged. "I knew he was careless with his assets and his investments, but I managed to curb some of his excesses while I was in control of his estates. I'm sure it was a large blow when Lord Rexford left and took his inheritance with him."

Rexford's smile held a hint of bitterness. "He'd been siphoning off money from my inheritance—the one that my mother left to me and to which he legally had no right. Thankfully, Clarence managed to move around some money and restore the funds my father stole."

"Indeed," Clarence said. "Which meant that Lord Sherbourne was already on the verge of finding himself in debt when his son took control of his inheritance."

I whistled. "It's a miracle that Sherbourne hasn't had you killed."

Clarence smiled. "I'm sure he wanted to, but I

know too much. Certain secrets would come out with my death that Sherbourne would do anything to keep hidden."

I turned to look at Rexford. "Do I need to know about these secrets?"

Rexford shrugged. "I don't even know what they are, but apparently, Clarence has made arrangements for them to become known if anything were to happen to him."

I nodded. I'd always known that Rexford trusted Clarence, but now, I understood why. It seemed that Rexford had only managed to gain his independence from his father's control because of his club manager's intervention.

I turned back to Brantford. "So, what do we do?"

Brantford steepled his fingers over his chest. "I'll have a talk with the man. As a liaison to the Crown, I can make it known that it would be in his best interest not to create further scandal with respect to his daughter."

"At this point, would he even care?" I asked.

"Father cares," Rexford said. "He cares very much. But more than that, he doesn't want anyone to learn about his financial constraints."

Brantford looked at his nails. "And on occasion,

I do have the opportunity to inform the Crown as to which of their aristocracy can be most relied upon. A few words in their ears, and Sherbourne would become a social pariah."

I gazed at the three men. "This all seems too easy. Should I go see him?"

"Absolutely not," Brantford said. "That is the last thing you should do. A baron going to see him, asking for his daughter's hand…" He shook his head. "I wouldn't want anything bad to befall you."

Ice slithered through my veins. Message received. Stay as far away from Victoria's father as possible. But I couldn't help feeling that I was still missing an important piece of the puzzle. "So, we return home and wait for you to tell us it's all been settled."

"Actually," Rexford said, "I will be returning home with Victoria. We must keep up appearances now, which means that since the townhouse is in my name, I will need to take up residence there."

One corner of Brantford's mouth lifted. "My wife has taken it upon herself to rehabilitate Lady Victoria's reputation. They will be seen about town together, and your intended will be living with her brother in his townhouse."

There was an edge to Brantford's words that told me he knew exactly what I was thinking. He knew very well that I didn't want to give Victoria up for even one day.

I looked at Rexford. "If you think this is for the best…"

Rexford nodded. "It is."

I released a harsh breath. "Fine. But I want to be the one to tell her." I rose to my feet, and the others followed suit. "Where can I find her?"

"I'm fairly certain that my wife has taken her to the exercise room."

My brows rose. "The exercise room?"

His eyes twinkled with amusement. "She and my sister have been teaching women of the ton how to defend themselves against improper advances and would-be assailants. It's become something of a pet project for them. I'm sure she wouldn't have been able to resist the temptation to take Lady Victoria under her tutelage right now, given everything that's happening."

I smiled at the man, my assessment of him increasing. He was even more impressive than I'd imagined.

Brantford rose and spoke to the footman

waiting in the hall. "Would you please show Baron Moreland to the exercise room?"

The butler bowed and, with a "Follow me, my lord," started down the hallway.

I obeyed, fascinated by what I would find.

CHAPTER 33

VICTORIA

I was sweating and out of breath as Lady Brantford watched me from a few feet away.

She shook her head. "No, you're standing all wrong. You must stand like this."

She arranged my body into what she deemed the proper stance, then illustrated what she wanted me to do. She moved with a twist and lowered one shoulder before flinging the large, heavy sack over her shoulder.

She straightened and faced me again. "You

cannot hesitate. If an assailant comes up behind you, they won't wait for you to decide what to do."

I shook my head, amazed. Of all the things that could have happened today, I never imagined that Lord Brantford's wife would begin to instruct me in the art of defending myself against an attacker.

"I'm not sure I can do that. I'm not very strong."

The countess smiled at me. "You don't need strength. You will have the element of surprise. Although…" She sighed and placed her hands on her hips. "I suspect that word is beginning to make its way among certain gentlemen. We might have to start instructing women on how to use blades."

I gaped at the woman. "Fencing blades?"

She smiled softly. "No, something smaller." She lifted the hem of her gown and showed me what, at first glance, appeared to be a garter. "This is what I mean. If I was leaving the house, I would have a small blade inserted here into this sheath. I also carry one in my reticule. But since I'm home today, I have no need." She shrugged and let the fabric fall.

I shook my head, amazed. "How is it possible that you—" My mouth snapped closed. "Of course. Lord Brantford."

"Yes." Rose smiled. "His sister, the Duchess of Castlefield, is quite adept as well. She took me under her wing when my husband started courting me. There were other… complications at the time, but that is all behind us. And since then, the two of us have been helping other women. It is horrible that we're left so defenseless out there. And often, the very men we expect to watch out for us are the ones from whom we need protection."

My mouth twisted to the side. "I can't see a situation where I would ever take a blade to my father."

She winced. "No, of course not." Her eyes narrowed as she watched me closely. "What if Moreland's life were in danger?"

My heart seized in my chest at the thought.

She nodded in understanding. "You don't have to kill anyone. Sometimes, just a small wound is sufficient to give you time to escape. But you must remember that when we get to that stage in our lessons, if you can't see yourself using a weapon, it is important not to carry one. Because if you did, then your assailant would have something to take and use against you."

My thoughts spun. "I'm going to be having lessons with you?"

She nodded. "And with my sister-in-law, of course."

"But I thought we were here to make other plans."

She smiled. "If you decide you want them, of course. I just thought that perhaps since you were at risk of being abducted, it would be good to show you a few things that might come in handy."

I straightened my shoulders and nodded. "Show me that movement again, then I will try tossing that sack over my shoulder."

Rose beamed. It was difficult to believe that I was on a first-name basis with the Countess of Brantford. My father outranked her husband, but everyone stood in awe of Lord Brantford.

"Follow my movements slowly, then I will watch you do it in normal speed. After, we can try it with one of the other bags around the room. I can toss one of them over my shoulder, but lifting one is something else entirely."

We did just that. I struggled a bit at first when I grabbed what was supposed to be an arm. And though the movement wasn't swift or as graceful as my instructor had shown me, I managed to send the life-sized sack flying over my shoulder and onto the ground in front of me.

A low whistle sounded from the door, and I turned to see Moreland leaning against the doorframe, watching us. I was suddenly aware of my unkempt hair, and my cheeks were no doubt red from the unaccustomed exertion.

"Tell me, my lady," he said, looking at the countess, "that you aren't teaching her how to maim me."

Rose laughed. "Of course not, my lord. Not unless you've decided to turn into a would-be assailant, of course."

His eyes met mine, and I blushed, thinking about some of the things we'd done in the bedroom. I hoped that the countess couldn't decipher that look.

He straightened and moved farther into the room. "We've decided on a plan." He looked at the countess. "Can I speak to Victoria alone for a moment?"

Rose smiled at me and squeezed my shoulder. "I'll meet you both back in the drawing room."

I watched her leave. Moreland bowed in her direction, then he closed the door behind her. When he faced me again, my stomach sank.

I rushed to his side. "What's the matter? Please tell me that you decided on a course of action that will allow us to marry. Or have you changed your mind?"

He silenced me with a short, hard kiss. "I am not changing my mind. But there is bad news."

I sucked in a deep breath and tried to calm my racing heart. Moreland hadn't changed his mind about marrying me. I didn't know why my thoughts kept jumping to that conclusion when he'd given me no reason to doubt him.

But that meant the bad news could only be one thing. "Will I have to hide away until I'm twenty-one? Or are we eloping?"

He shook his head. "Neither. Your father has financial difficulties. Your brother and Brantford have decided that he would agree to anything to keep that information from becoming known."

I nodded. "He would. But I must say that I'm shocked. I had no idea he was having financial constraints."

"No one does," Moreland said. "He hid it well. And that is why he wanted you to marry Lord Heddington. Because instead of giving Heddington the customary dowry, your father intended to accept a large sum of money from him."

I paled at that information. "If that's true, Father won't want to give up on his plan."

Moreland's expression was fierce. "He won't have a choice. I won't give you up, and in no reality will you marry Heddington."

My breath caught in my throat. Moreland's eyes blazed with determination, and I was viscerally aware of just how handsome he was. Beyond that, I could clearly see how dedicated he was to ensuring we marry. He wanted this, and I wanted him. Even if he never loved me, it was enough that he cared about me.

I nodded. "So, what is this bad news you wanted to tell me?"

He winced. "Your brother is moving into the townhouse, and I'm moving out."

My mouth dropped open.

"We will rehabilitate your image now, Victoria —erasing all our attempts to ruin you. That is the only way we can move forward with a marriage without eloping to Scotland."

"But—" I started.

He traced my lower lip with his thumb, and my protest died.

"I know," he said. "I hate it as well. But I will get a special license so we can wed quickly."

I leaned into him, holding onto his shoulders. "I

don't want a large society wedding that will take weeks to plan."

He smiled down at me. "I don't think anyone expects a Legend's wedding to be a society affair. They would expect something private."

I nodded. "That makes sense. Of course, they're going to think that you ruined me and that I am with child."

He reached down and placed his large hand over my belly. "You might be."

A shiver of happiness raced through me at the thought.

"But it doesn't matter. With Brantford on our side and with your brother's connections, no one will shun you. You'll hardly be the first society miss to give birth eight months after marrying."

He kissed me then, and I sank into him. All my fears for the future vanished. The only thing I cared about was being with Moreland.

CHAPTER 34

VICTORIA

The details about what would happen next were decided quickly. Lord Branford would call on my father later in the day to explain that Moreland and I had his support for our upcoming union.

While I knew that Lord Branford had a lot of power, under normal circumstances, his support wouldn't have swayed Father from his desire to see me wed to Lord Heddington. But Lord Brantford's threat to make it known that Father was teetering on the verge of bankruptcy would be a powerful threat. I was shocked to learn that my father had spent the money set aside for my dowry and had already sold one of his unentailed estates.

I wasn't sure their threats to expose him would be enough to convince Father, but I remained hopeful.

Rexford suggested that we ask our father to call on us at King's. But I suggested we invite him to visit us at the townhouse. I'd grown comfortable in the home that Moreland and I had made for each other in the past few days.

When I returned to that house, it was my brother who accompanied me. It made sense, after all. We'd come up with the original plan to ruin my reputation, but now we had to reverse course. The townhouse was Rexford's, so the story would be spread that I was staying with my brother. When I asked about all those times Moreland had visited the house, Rexford had shrugged and said, "He was merely visiting a friend."

I knew that his assurances wouldn't stop the gossips, but society would move on quickly enough when the next scandal broke. And if life had one constant, it was that there was always another scandal.

We entered the house, and I stepped aside as Rexford explained to the staff that he would be spending the night in Moreland's room. Since the baron would be returning to his own townhouse, there would be no need to set up another bedroom.

I turned away, my cheeks heating. The staff knew that Moreland had been spending the night with me recently, so his room was already clean. I was sure Rexford would know that, but I wasn't about to mention it.

Rexford took me into the drawing room and settled next to me on the settee. "It is not too late to change your mind about inviting him here. We both know how unpleasant Sherbourne can be, and I would spare you his anger. I can ask him to meet me at the club tomorrow. You don't have to be there."

I bit my lip as I considered his offer. I would be lying if I said I wasn't tempted, but in the end, I shook my head. "I need to be there, and I feel most comfortable here, with Moreland and you by my side. It is time for me to stop running away from Father. I've been hiding from his wrath my whole life, but that ends now."

He stared at me for several seconds, and I knew he was searching for any sign of doubt on my part. But I was determined to see this through. If I wanted to marry Moreland, it was time to become worthy of him. He had risked much to save me from my father. I needed to show him that I could stand by his side.

I knew the meeting would be unpleasant. I had witnessed my father set others in their place. He would be vicious to Moreland, and I had to be there to show my support.

Finally, Rexford nodded. "I'm proud of you."

I laughed. "Did you know it would come to this?"

His smile held hidden depths. "Come to what?"

I huffed out a breath. I didn't know my brother that well. He'd left for school when I was still young, and whenever he'd visited between school terms, he'd been aloof and distant. I knew it was because Father had done everything in his power to control his son and make him into little more than an extension of himself.

I didn't know how Rexford managed to gain his independence and find the funds to set up his own club. I suspected that Mr. Clarence had helped him since he was no longer Father's steward and was now managing Rexford's club.

But the fact that Rexford had installed people within my father's household whose sole purpose was to see to my welfare meant that he'd worried about me. And he hadn't hesitated to help me when I'd come to him.

"Did you suspect that in the end, I would need to marry?"

I could see Rexford weighing his words. "I'd hoped that it would be enough to ruin you, but Sherbourne is stubborn. It was always possible that you might have to marry, but it was equally possible that I would have to find a way to hide you up north."

I nodded. "And Moreland?"

He shrugged. "I was willing to be led by you in this, but I must say, I'm glad you chose him."

I shivered at that. Did Rexford actually approve of our upcoming marriage? "I know about his reputation with women."

Rexford winced. "We all have something of a reputation. But Moreland…" He shook his head. "Moreland is loyal. When he gives you his word, he won't break it."

"Are you saying that your other friends aren't loyal?"

"They're loyal to me, of course, and to each other."

"But?" I prodded when he hesitated.

"I don't know. I've always had this feeling that

Moreland, of all of us, would be the first to wed. Of course I'd expected him to wed out of convenience. But with you…" His gaze settled on me, searching. He seemed to be trying to read my thoughts. "He cares about you."

I took a deep breath. "I care about him as well." My voice lowered. "I love him."

Rexford's smile softened. "I'm glad to hear that."

"Do you think it's possible that he might…?"

Rexford's expression was impassive. "That's a question you will have to ask him."

I shook my head. "I suppose it doesn't really matter. He assured me that he's not marrying me out of a sense of responsibility, but how can I be certain? As you said, he did give you his word that he would look after me."

He took my hands and squeezed them. "I released him from his promise, Victoria. I told him that I would send you away and Brantford has the means to ensure you are never found. Between the two of us, you would be free. And if Moreland wanted his freedom, he could have had it."

My breath hitched. "So you think there's a chance for the two of us?"

"I think you'll have to ask him about his feelings

for you. But I can tell you that Moreland would call out any man who tried to take you from him. I think it's safe to assume he's not merely acting out of a sense of duty to me."

My heart raced. Even if Moreland didn't love me, my brother's words did much to assure me that he cared. It would have to be enough.

CHAPTER 35

After Victoria and her brother climbed into the carriage, I couldn't stand to watch her leave without me. So I turned to walk away.

It was not yet evening when I returned to my empty townhouse. I'd always enjoyed the solitude that came with living alone, but the house seemed unnaturally still. I couldn't help but feel as though I no longer belonged there. I belonged wherever Victoria was.

So little time had passed since Victoria had come to King's to see Rexford, yet my life was forever changed. I was no longer the man who never spent more than one night with the same woman. That man would have felt trapped by the situation in which I found myself. I was not yet thirty, after all, and before this week, I hadn't given serious consideration to the idea of marrying. By all accounts, I should be dreading my upcoming nuptials.

But while I found myself filled with anxiety, it wasn't because I was about to lose the freedom that came with bachelorhood. I was unsettled because Victoria wasn't here with me.

I made my way to the study and headed straight for the sideboard, where I kept my brandy. After pouring a healthy measure, I sank into an armchair. I had to pace myself. Tomorrow, we would meet with Victoria's father, and I had to perform my part. Victoria was already lowering herself by marrying a mere baron. I wouldn't embarrass her further by attending that meeting while suffering from the obvious aftereffects of having indulged in too much alcohol. So I slowly drank the one glass I would allow myself while I tortured myself with thoughts of how much I wanted to race to her side. It seemed impossible that Rexford's sister could become so important to me in such a short time.

I smiled as I recalled that first moment when

our eyes had met at King's. Never had I felt such an immediate and visceral attraction to a woman before. Was this fate? Were we always meant to be together?

I tossed back the last of the brandy and reclined in the chair. I closed my eyes, settled my hands on my waist, and ordered myself to think about anything but Victoria. Instead, scenes played in my mind's eye of all the time we'd spent together. The conversations we'd had, how adorable she'd looked that first day when she'd been playing with her paints. I hadn't told her that she had a splash of red paint on her cheek. But seeing it there had made me content because it meant that I'd made her happy. I'd given her something that she so clearly enjoyed and that had been kept from her. I would spend the rest of my life trying to make her happy. That thought should have terrified me. Instead it filled me with pleasure.

Neither of us wanted a large society wedding. As soon as tomorrow's meeting was over, I would procure a special license. One way or another, Victoria Wright would soon be my wife. I couldn't spend another day away from her. But for tonight, I needed to inform the staff that they should prepare my home to receive the next Baroness Moreland.

CHAPTER 36

MORELAND

Anticipation surged through my veins the following morning when I woke. The sensation wasn't dissimilar to the way I felt before beginning a match at Gentleman Jackson's. I wasn't about to engage in a physical fight, but I was most definitely going into battle. Instead of fists, the weapons would be words and displays of power.

I took great care when dressing, choosing my most expensive watch fob and adding a diamond stick pin in my cravat. My waistcoat was made from a rich blue silk, and my tailcoat and trousers had been procured from the most sought-after tailor on

Bond Street. In terms of social status, I was beneath Victoria. She was a duke's daughter, and I was merely a baron, but I would not be an embarrassment to her today.

I left the house just before noon. Rexford had sent word that the meeting was scheduled for one o'clock in the afternoon. I knew that he liked to wake early in the morning, and Victoria seemed to share that habit, but I purposely chose not to arrive too soon.

I'd learned over the years that before beginning a boxing match, it was important not to show a hint of weakness. I feared that arriving too early would be a disservice to Victoria. I was sure she would be prepared for the meeting. I'd witnessed firsthand the way Rexford could infuse those around him with his calm confidence, whereas with me, she tended to confide her deepest fears. I didn't want her dwelling on what could go wrong before her father arrived. Much as I'd hated it, Rexford had been correct in sending me away last night. My nervous energy would have undermined the calm demeanor we all needed to project.

I took note of the fact that Rexford still had men watching the house. I waved to them casually and let myself into the townhouse. Two footmen stood in the hallway, their muscles tense and ready for action. They relaxed when they saw me.

I nodded to them and turned into the drawing room. Relief swept through me when I saw Victoria. She sat on the edge of the settee, her hands folded in her lap, wearing a demure pale-yellow gown that I knew her father would approve of. Like the footmen in the hallway, her muscles were tense. When she saw me, she leaped to her feet and rushed into my arms. Relief flooded me as I drew her close.

Only then did I notice that Rexford was also in the room. He leaned back in an armchair, his arms folded over his chest, one brow raised as he watched us.

I turned back to Victoria and dropped a kiss on her temple. "It will be over soon."

She nodded against my chest, then took a deep breath, as though filling her lungs with my scent, before stepping away. "Yes. Father likes to be early. He says it sets his opponents on edge."

Of course it would. We lived in a society where people liked to roll out of bed in the middle of the afternoon. Arriving early would ensure that his opponents weren't at their best. I felt a moment of panic. "He hasn't…"

Rexford shook his head. "No. He should realize that we'd be prepared for his usual antics."

Victoria glanced at her brother. "The meeting was set for two o'clock, but since it is almost one o'clock, I expect—"

Someone knocked at the door.

"There he is." Rexford rose to his feet. "Still up to his same old tricks."

Victoria smiled at me. "I'm glad you're here."

I kissed her quickly. "I wouldn't be anywhere else."

She beamed up at me, then moved back to the settee.

I wanted to sit next to her, but we weren't yet betrothed. Instead, I went to stand next to Rexford. "Everything is in order?"

Rexford nodded. The front door opened, and moments later, the Duke of Sherbourne stepped into the drawing room. No one was surprised that he hadn't waited to be announced.

His gaze moved over the inhabitants of the room, his jaw tightening when he settled on Victoria. "You've given me a great deal of trouble."

I watched the way her face betrayed not a hint of emotion at her father's words. She was used to being berated by him, after all.

He looked at Rexford next. "I expected nothing less from you."

Then his contemptuous regard fell on me. "I'd hoped we could discuss this matter without complications being present."

I kept my muscles loose. If he thought I was merely a complication, he had vastly underestimated me. He moved into the room, leaning heavily on his cane, and settled onto the settee.

I noticed the imperceptible tightening of Victoria's fingers on her lap before she forced herself to loosen them.

Sherbourne pulled a folded note from his pocket. "I received a visit from Lord Brantford yesterday evening. I must say, you've all unnecessarily muddled this entire situation." He turned to look at Victoria. "Apparently, you were successful in keeping your delicate sensibilities hidden from me. I'd assumed that the daughter I raised knew her place. But clearly, you inherited the same defect as your brother, choosing to run away instead of staying and performing your duties." He dropped the note on the settee between him and his daughter. "I've taken the opportunity to compose a list of suitable candidates for your hand in marriage. I don't understand why you're against Lord Heddington, but I'm sure you will find someone suitable on that list."

Victoria's eyes fell on the paper, then she looked up at me.

Sherbourne scowled. "If your qualms are with his age, you'll find a wide variety of suitable gentlemen listed. You can have anyone you want. You don't need to settle for a baron."

He didn't even look at me when he said the word. In his mind, I was a nonentity. Victoria continued to look at me.

I smiled at her. "Take a look at the note, Victoria. Your father won't be satisfied until he realizes that there is no one you would rather have."

Her gaze stayed on me for several seconds, then she looked at Rexford. Her brother nodded. She reached for the note and unfolded it before scanning the list.

"As you can see, I've taken your delicate sensibilities into consideration." Sherbourne's voice dripped with disapproval. "I will see to it that any of those men are made aware that you would be open to a courtship. I'm sure, given everything that you have learned of late, that you wouldn't find it difficult to entice one into offering for you."

My fists curled at my side, and I took a step

forward, ready to call this man out for impugning his daughter in such a way. Rexford grabbed my arm and stopped me.

"And what about your financial situation?" he said. "Would those men care that you don't have the money for Victoria's dowry?"

Sherbourne shrugged. "I have a few unentailed estates. It would be a simple matter to sell one of them."

I clasped my hands behind my back, trying to control my fury, but Rexford was right. I needed to maintain the appearance of calm.

That didn't mean I had to remain silent. "I, on the other hand, wouldn't need to sell any of my holdings. Nor do I require a dowry. I have more than enough money to provide for your daughter."

"You've done enough." Sherbourne rose to his feet, his face mottled with anger. "Victoria is far above your reach, and you cannot have her."

"Enough." Victoria stood and faced her father, the list clutched in her hands. "The decision is mine. I have given your suggestions my careful consideration, and I must decline your offer."

Then she tore the list in two and tossed it back onto the settee.

CHAPTER 37

VICTORIA

I shook when my father turned his anger on me, but I refused to look away. I'd been under his thumb my entire life. I'd given him everything he'd ever demanded without protest, but this was a step too far. I couldn't allow Father to speak to Moreland in such a way, not when he'd shown me more kindness and understanding in the last week than I'd known my entire life.

"This is my last warning," Father said. "Give up this nonsense and—" He halted, realizing that nothing he could say would convince me to go with him.

We both knew that once I was under his roof again, he would move forward with the original betrothal to Lord Heddington. He'd never shown any care for my desires and wouldn't start now.

I squared my shoulders. "I would rather be this man's mistress than marry any other man."

Father's eyes narrowed, and I felt a moment of real fear.

Fortunately, Rexford stepped in. "It's over, Sherbourne."

Our father flinched at the title coming from his son's lips.

Father turned his glare on Rexford. "You've taken far too many liberties."

Rexford's voice was steady, a fact that seemed only to increase our father's anger. "Quite frankly, I don't have to justify my actions to you."

The expression on my father's face was one that normally would have had me cowering. But not here and not now, standing in unity with my brother and the man I loved. I had to be strong for them, show Moreland that I was worthy of his respect, even if he would never come to love me.

Father turned to face me. "Don't expect me at the wedding." He made his way from the room, leaning heavily on his cane. He stopped in the doorway but didn't turn to face us. "You two have been my biggest disappointments."

We watched him leave without another word. I held my breath, half expecting him to return.

The silence was broken by Rexford's vehement "Good riddance."

I turned to face him. "Is that all? Am I free?"

Rexford shrugged. "It would appear that way, but I think it best if we maintain security around the house."

I turned to Moreland. "Are you…?" I swallowed and asked Rexford my question. "Are you staying here tonight?"

Rexford looked at his friend, then back at me. "I think I'll return to the club tonight. I trust Moreland to keep you safe."

He clapped a hand on Moreland's shoulder, and a wordless exchange passed between them. Then Rexford followed our father from the house.

I turned to look at Moreland, who hadn't said a word for some time. He wore an odd expression, and my stomach sank.

"I apologize about everything my father said. None of it is true. You're worth more than all those other men combined, even if you no longer want to have anything to do with me." My breath hitched, but I forced myself to continue. "I would understand why you wouldn't want to align yourself with the Duke of Sherbourne. He would be your father-in-law, after all, and I'm sure he'd be an even worse father-in-law than he is a father." I wrapped my arms around my waist.

Moreland continued to stare at me in silence, and I couldn't hold back.

"Say something. Tell me what you're thinking."

Moreland's eyes roved over my face. When he spoke, his voice was low. "You chose me."

I couldn't understand his tone of incredulity. "Of course, I chose you. I love you." My hand flew to my mouth at the admission. Then I sank onto the settee and hid my face in my hands. "I know that love wasn't part of our arrangement. I know that you've never been in a long-term relationship, and I understand that any marriage between us would be a practical one. I wouldn't expect more from you than you're willing to give."

I felt him settle next to me, and I wanted to cry.

He took hold of my wrists and pulled my hands away from my face. "You love me?"

My smile was tremulous. I took heart from that fact that he didn't seem angry at my admission. "You can hardly blame me. You've been my knight in shining armor. You're handsome. You're intelli-gent. You make me laugh. And you've never treated me like a burden. I'm sure every woman you've been with would give everything they possess to be in my shoes."

He smiled. "I don't care about anyone else, Victoria, because it's you I love."

I was convinced that my foolish heart had caused me to mishear him. "Did you just say you love me?"

His smile broadened, and his hand came up to cup my cheek. "Is that so hard to believe? You barged into my life, and from the first moment I saw you..." He shook his head. "I can't explain it, but I wanted you even then. And last night, when I couldn't stand the idea of being away from you, I finally realized why."

I couldn't hold back a scoff. "From what I've heard, you want many women."

"No, Victoria, I didn't just want you. I needed you. Not just for the night. There was something about you. When you turned and our eyes met, I felt as though you could see right into my soul."

A tear rolled down my face. "And you're roman-tic. I never stood a chance."

He laughed, wiping away the tear with his

thumb. "Apparently, I'm a bit of a fool when it comes to you."

I threw myself into his arms. He lifted me onto his lap, and we stayed like that for several minutes. His arms wrapped around me, my face against his neck as I clung to him.

"I can't believe you love me."

I must have said the words aloud because he kissed my temple. "I love you, Victoria Wright. Never doubt it. It's not an emotion I ever expected to feel. If you had agreed to marry one of those other men, I don't think I could have allowed it."

I lifted my head and gazed up at him. "Good, because I only want you."

His mouth crashed against mine, and we kissed as though we'd been apart for far longer than one night.

"I'll get a special license," he said between kisses. His mouth roved down to my jawline, and he trailed kisses along the side of my throat. "But not just yet. Right now, I think the two of us have some celebrating to do."

"Whatever you say, my lord. But first, perhaps we should close the drawing room door."

He laughed, then picked me up and carried me upstairs to our bedroom.

EPILOGUE 1

VICTORIA

*W*e were married two days later in a private ceremony. It was the exact opposite of the type of society affair my father would have insisted upon if he'd had his way. And it was everything I could have wanted.

The Legends all attended—Viscount Fairfax, the Earl of Clifton, Viscount Kendrick, the Earl of Greyson, and my brother, Rexford. Mr. Clarence was also there. He wasn't a Legend, but he was an essential part of the group.

The Earl and Countess of Brantford were also in attendance, as were the Duke and Duchess of

Castlefield. Along with officially forming the School of Defense for Young Women, the duchess and countess had decided to ensure I was welcomed back into society with open arms.

I had a feeling that it would be a relatively easy undertaking. When word of our betrothal spread, I received an avalanche of calling cards and invitations to upcoming events as well as notes of felicitation.

Only two days had passed since that meeting with my father, and I was astounded at just how quickly that piece of gossip had spread. But I shouldn't have been surprised. I'd accomplished the impossible, after all. I'd married a Legend.

King's was closed for the private wedding breakfast. True to his word, my father hadn't attended the ceremony. Instead, he'd left town on a fabricated emergency at one of his estates. With him gone and my husband standing by my side, I felt truly free for the first time in my life.

Moreland leaned down to drop a kiss on my temple. "What are you thinking?"

I smiled up at him. "I never expected to feel so happy. Rexford was away at school for most of the year, and after he gained his independence, I rarely saw him. My father was never more to me than a disapproving taskmaster. But this…"

My gaze swept over the people present to celebrate our marriage. They chatted and laughed amiably in small groups. Lord Fairfax met my gaze and raised a glass of champagne in a silent toast to us.

My smile widened, and tears stung my eyes. "This feels like I finally have a family."

Moreland kissed me, soft and light. I didn't have to look around to know that everyone was watching us.

"You will always have me. But know that everyone here would lay down their lives for you." He reached into a pocket and drew out a sovereign coin. "Only six of these were made originally, but now there is a seventh medallion. Welcome to the Legends. You're one of us now."

He placed the heavy gold medallion in my hand, and I realized it wasn't a sovereign. On one side was a raised crown, the emblem for Rexford's club, King's. I turned it over to find a raised six-point star, each point long and narrow. Six points for the six Legendary Lords of the ton.

Emotion clogged my throat as I moved into Moreland's arms.

I was finally home.

EPILOGUE 2

THE MAYFAIR CHRONICLE

Hell hath frozen over.

One of the Legendary Lords has done the unthinkable and taken a wife. Even more surprising are the rumors that suggest this is a love match. Our astonished but sincere felicitations go out to Baron Moreland and his bride, Lady Victoria Moreland.

I wonder if this is the beginning of a new era for the Legends…

MORELAND

Lying in bed, I pulled Victoria more firmly against me and trailed a hand along her arm. She sighed, the soft sound filled with contentment, and turned her head to drop a kiss on my chest.

She smiled at me and my heart expanded. It amazed me that we were married, and I vowed silently that I would spend the rest of my life proving I was worthy of her love.

She started making lazy circles on my chest, and her light touch caused me to harden. Again. "You seem deep in thought."

That was an understatement. The day's events had been surreal. First, the wedding ceremony in the small chapel that was attended by the Legends and by the Brantfords and Castlefields. They were a new alliance that Victoria's brother had cultivated.

Rexford was known for his strategic alliances, so I wasn't surprised. He hadn't told me what Brantford had asked of him in exchange for helping us with the Duke of Sherbourne. But I knew that whatever the price, Rexford would willingly pay it to keep his sister safe. As would I.

My gaze roamed over her beautiful face. "It seems incredible to me that the first wedding I've ever attended would be my own."

Her eyes danced with amusement. "I hope I won't be too much of a burden."

I could tell she was thinking about the vigorous rounds of lovemaking in which we'd just engaged. After the wedding breakfast at King's, I hadn't been able to wait until we were home and so we'd consummated our marriage in the carriage. But now we were safely tucked away in my townhouse —or rather, *our* townhouse—and hadn't left the bedroom since our arrival.

"I should call for dinner trays to be brought up.

I'm afraid I might have worn you out." I vowed to do that soon, but I couldn't bring myself to release Victoria just yet.

Her hand coasted down my body, and I sucked in a breath when she encircled my cock and began stroking me. I was fully hard within seconds.

"Are you sure that's what you want to do, Matthew?"

Pleasure filled me. She usually called me by my title, and I was surprised at how much I liked hearing her use my given name.

"I don't think it's a secret that I'm always hard when you're near."

She bit her lip, and I noticed the hint of color on her cheeks. I traced the dusting of pink with a thumb.

"Are you embarrassed?"

She grimaced, and her hand returned to my chest. "We've been in your bedroom for hours and the sun has only just set. I don't think I'll ever be able to face your staff again."

I couldn't help but laugh. "They'll think you bewitched me. They were delighted when I told them I would be marrying soon, and I could tell they were all enchanted with you today."

I rolled us until I hovered over her. She cupped my face, her gaze turning soft. Unable to ignore the impulse, I turned my head to take one of her fingers into my mouth and pulled gently on it.

Her eyes widened, and she freed her hand. "Why does that feel so good?"

I grinned down at her. "There is one thing I'd love you to do before we ring for dinner."

Her nose scrunched in that delightful way she had when she was confused. Clearly, I would have to give her a bigger hint.

I put my thumb against her lips. "Suck on it, Victoria."

Her brow wrinkled as she followed my instructions. Heat streaked through me, and I couldn't hold back my groan.

Her eyes widened then, and I knew she'd worked out what I was suggesting. To my delight, she gave my thumb a few more pulls with her wonderful mouth before releasing it with a soft pop.

She was going to kill me.

"You are wicked, my lord."

I grinned. "And you are amazing."

Victoria laughed as she urged me onto my back and started kissing her way down my body. When she reached my cock, she didn't even hesitate before taking it into her mouth. I put one hand on her head, guiding her gently. I would never take more than she was willing to give.

I shouldn't have been surprised that she quickly proved herself quite adept at the task at hand and sent up silent thanks to the fates, who had seen fit to bring Victoria into my life.

And then all thought disappeared as I gave myself over to bliss.

Thank you for reading *Ruined by the Baron*! I hope you love Victoria and Moreland as much as I do.

The next book in the Legendary Lords series, *Won by the Viscount*, tells Viscount Kendrick's story. It is available for pre-order now.

Won by the Viscount

When I win a rare jewel in a card game, I don't expect it to be the diamond of the Season.

Even more disturbing is the fact that I want to keep her.

⸻

To LEARN about new books and to gain access to my bonus content, sign up to my newsletter: suzannamedeiros.com/newsletter.

USA Today bestselling author Suzanna Medeiros was born and raised in Toronto, Canada. Her love for the written word led her to pursue a degree in English Literature from the University of Toronto. She went on to earn a Bachelor of Education degree before deciding to pursue her first love—writing.

Suzanna is married to her own hero and survived raising twins. When she isn't writing she loves reading, watching science fiction, and playing video games.

She would like to thank her parents for showing her that love at first sight and happily ever after really do exist.

To learn more about Suzanna's books, you can visit her website at www.suzannamedeiros.com.

To learn when she has a new release available, you can sign up for her mailing list at suzannamedeiros.com/newsletter.

instagram.com/suzannamedeiros

facebook.com/AuthorSuzannaMedeiros

bookbub.com/profile/suzanna-medeiros

goodreads.com/suzannamedeiros

BOOKS BY SUZANNA MEDEIROS

Legendary Lords of the Ton series:

Ruined by the Baron

Won by the Viscount (coming soon)

Landing a Lord series:

Dancing with the Duke

Loving the Marquess

Beguiling the Earl

The Unaffected Earl

The Unsuitable Duke

The Unexpected Marquess

The Unwilling Viscount

The Baron's Return

Courting the Earl

Tempting the Viscount

Christmas Scandals series:

A Viscount for Christmas

A Highwayman for Christmas

A Rogue for Christmas

A Betrothal for Christmas (coming soon)

Hathaway Heirs series:

Lady Hathaway's Proposal

Lord Hathaway's Bride

Captain Hathaway's Dilemma

Miss Hathaway's Wish

Single Titles:

Dear Stranger

Forbidden in February

Anthologies:

The Novellas: A Collection

Hathaway Heirs: Books 1-4

Landing a Lord: Books 1-3

Landing a Lord: Books 4-6

Landing a Lord: Books 7-9

Christmas Scandals: Books 1-3

For more information and an up-to-date book list please visit the author's website: https://www.suzannamedeiros. com/books/

www.ingramcontent.com/pod-product-compliance
Lightning Source LLC
Chambersburg PA
CBHW021023310726
48969CB00006B/1514